FAE'S WOLF
FATED MATES OF THE FAE ROYALS, SUMMER COURT BOOK 2
HELEN WALTON

Walton House Publishing

CONTENTS

FOREWORD

AUTHOR NOTE

Choosing character names is not always easy, and there are times you pick them to mean something for the character and the story. I've included the pronunciation and meaning of the names, and if you're like me, and like to know and still pronounce the names the way you read them, then welcome to my club.

Niamh pronounced neeve meaning radiance.

Fintan pronounced fin-tan meaning white fire.

Eamon pronounced aim-on meaning keeper of riches.

Maeve pronounced may-veh meaning intoxicating.

Diarmuid pronounced deer-mid meaning without enemy.

Orlaith pronounced or-lah meaning golden princess.

Rian pronounced ree-an means little king

Briana pronounced bree-a-nah meaning noble.

Aislinn pronounced ash-lin meaning a vision or dream

Saoirse pronounced seer-sha meaning freedom.

Lorcan pronounced lor-can meaning silent or fierce.

Ciara pronounced kee-ra meaning dark

Roisin pronounced row-sheen meaning little rose.

Deirdre pronounced deer-dree meaning broken-hearted.

Malachi pronounced mal-lah-key means messenger of God.

Tadhg pronounced tie-guh meaning poet or philosopher.

For the power of freedom is in love.

CHAPTER ONE
SAOIRSE
THE SUMMER COURT

T HE CHANGE IN THE Fae Kingdom was noticeable over the last two hundred and seventy years. Water trickled from the spring into the pool beneath where once the stream had flourished. The Summer Court was no longer the thriving, joyful place it once was. Fluffy white blooms hanging from the atrium ceiling grew fewer and fewer each year, allowing the light from the sun and moon to shine inside in a glaring brightness. A deep unease rippled through my powers as my hand coaxed the pool into a swirling vortex. As though I could draw more water. More life force to our kingdom.

Yet, the task was impossible, even though I was a Fae royal. We controlled, wielded, and manipulated nature with our powers. Another magic regulated our spring of life, the Spring Baile, located in the heart of the Fae palace. Magic shrouded in so much secrecy even we didn't know where it originated.

The locked veil shimmered and thrummed against my palm. A reminder we could no longer pass between the Summer Court and Earth. Except... us royals could. I summoned more power, focusing on the massive force sealing us in.

"Saoirse," King Fintan, my father said.

A tiny jolt jerked inside my stomach, but I kept my face impassive and my palm still as I drew my power back from the lock. The Fae King couldn't learn I was about to slip through the veil.

"We've all tried to make the Spring Baile flourish, tis not a task our powers can accomplish," King Fintan said.

"I can't give up. We can't give up. It's our royal duty to protect the spring," I said. "Without the spring, we will die."

The Fae King's brows furrowed as he stared at the quickening maelstrom of my powers. Every Fae knew our immortality was connected to the life-giving and healing powers of the spring's water.

"Enough," he said, placing his hand on my shoulder.

I snapped my hand out of the water, flicking droplets over his robes. "Why won't you consider the locked veil might be the cause?"

His fingers tightened on my shoulder. "You cannot possibly entertain the notion I'd unlock the veil?"

"Time has passed, Father. You and Lorcan vanquished the Trappers. What do we have to be so afraid of on Earth?"

"No, Saoirse." He spun away and stalked the length of the atrium, his feet stomping over the cobblestones. "It's too much to ask. I can't and won't risk our people, my children, my mate again."

After the atrocities humans inflicted on the Fae, Father had used his enormous powers over all the elements to seal the veil between the two worlds, ensuring he'd protected the last of the Fae from harm. A protection King Fintan enforced with unwavering resolve, a sharp sword, and the Palace Guards. Soldiers who'd stood by him as they'd eliminated the human Trappers who'd massacred many Fae, including his parents. Soldiers who were loyal to the King and his will. And the King's will was firm that no Fae would leave the safety of the Summer Court.

Ever.

I inhaled a deep breath until my lungs filled with the calming aroma of the flowering vines.

"Besides." He returned to my side. "I came to talk to you about Tadhg."

"No." I scowled, already knowing the direction this talk would head.

"Why won't you consider taking him as your mate? I want you to be happy."

A strangled laugh left my lips. "I won't be happy with a chosen mate. I want what you and Mother have."

He threw his hands up in the air, his silver hair rippling with the force of his movements. "How do you know you won't be happy unless you try?"

"I don't wish to trade memories with Tadhg when I mark him as my mate. And I don't want to lie in the Quiet with him while I absorb his memories." I almost shuddered at the notion of falling into what humans called a coma for however long while the Fae mating process lasted beside Tadhg. "I most certainly don't want to share my memories with him."

His indigo-rimmed eyes snapped to mine. "I understand your hesitation. I'm sorry, but this is the only choice."

We stared at each other, neither of us willing to budge on our stances. I wished for a fated mate and a love like my parents shared. Father yearned for all his children to be happy and safe. Yet he was unwilling to unlock the veil separating Earth and the Summer Court. After the brutalities of the Trappers burning the Fae alive, I understood his motivation.

We had lost so many Fae, my grandparents, my niece, and almost my mother. The loss had almost been too much to withstand. For me. For all of us. But most of all, Mother and Father who'd become King and Queen of the Fae in the aftermath of the Fae burnings.

A fact we never talked about. It was easier to pretend those dark days didn't exist, but they did. They'd placed us where we were today. Locked behind the veil separating the Summer Court and Earth. Safe in our world from the humans who'd attempted to take our powers. Forever stuck in the one place with the same Fae for hundreds of years.

How were we supposed to find a fated mate?

The longer I kept his stare, the faster the Fae King's crown of thorns writhed around his head, as though he knew the dark direction of my thoughts. As though he saw the flames and charred bodies once again.

He rubbed a hand across his forehead, breaking the staring contest. "Come, child. Let us spar."

My eyebrows rose. "Now?"

"I believe we both have tension we'd like to relieve."

I blew out a breath. "Aye."

He left the atrium and strode into the great hallways. His regal robes fluttered as he turned toward the courtyard.

I cast a longing glance at the spring before following Father. The thumping of my heart quickened, making my chest ache as the thrill of impending combat swarmed through my body. Each step through the listless castle fed a deep-seated fear I wouldn't escape ever again if Father discovered his children could unlock the veil. We'd never be able to visit the forbidden world of Earth, the realm Father was trying to protect us from. The place the Fae shouldn't want to go.

My desires told me to flee the sanctuary, which was more like a prison these days.

We passed under the sparkling crystalline arches of the castle, but the light bouncing off them brought me no joy. Though the palace had been my home for hundreds of years, I'd never felt more uncertain of my future. The parquetry flooring of the courtyard warmed the soles of my cool feet, but it wouldn't warm my heart. Nothing and no one would but a mate.

As I padded to a stop in the center of the yard, my dress settled against my legs in one last swish. Father spun in a billowing swirl of his aquamarine robes. The crown of white-gold thorns writhed around his head as though alive and excited about the upcoming sparring match with his daughter.

"Water swords."

He clapped his hands together, emitting a loud boom across the room. Father extended his arms to reveal a sword of water in his firm grasp. The azure blue of the blade glistened under the sunlight streaming in through the open rooftop. I loved the sight of the blades, the way they swung through the air with a whistle, their sharpness and strength. My power rustled in excitement to be let loose in its favorite way. King Fintan tilted his head to the side.

My powers were astounding over water, but Father's were beyond the greatest realm of power and control as the crowned Fae King. With a wave of my hands, a short sword of azure water sprung to life in my palm. The hilt was heavy in my grasp. My knuckles whitened as my anger built. Why would he never consider opening the veil? He'd eradicated the Trappers.

I could have slipped through the veil with Father being none the wiser if he hadn't walked into the atrium. I'd be on the other side trying to find a cure for the spring. We needed to find one. It was our royal duty.

Perhaps if I won our sword fight, he might listen to me about the veil. But I'd never won a sword fight against the King. He was renowned for his impressive Fae powers and his sword fighting skills, too. At least he'd taught me his skills, trained me in the old ways of combat.

I'd never beat him, but I'd try.

Father lunged without warning and swung low. I countered with a quick block of my water sword, sending a thump through the courtyard, and ducked left. He flung his robes out behind him. I swung at his stomach, but he leaned back too quick for my strike and raised his eyebrows. I puffed out a breath and swung my sword up high. He counteracted with ease. A smirk stretched his pale lips as though he discerned the strike I'd used to attack. I lunged forward as a red-hot blast of ire filled my veins. He stepped back in a hurry. My heart raced in triumph and adrenaline shot through my limbs.

Father spun again in a twirl of blinding turquoise robes, dropped to his knees, and swung at me. I punched him in the face with my fist and the hilt of the sword. He spat bright red blood from his mouth onto the parquetry floor. I swung again. He blocked the arc of my blade with a thump of his solid water sword, setting my ears ringing to the loud reverberations, and kneed me in the ribcage. I stumbled back with the force of his blow, clenching my aching side. My breath wheezed in and out while my body repaired itself.

King Fintan walked around me as I struggled to regain my breath.

"You'll never beat me, Saoirse."

I glared up at the King while hunched over. My shoulders sagged. Every breath tasted like failure.

"If I win, will you consider opening the veil?"

"When I win this fight, will you consider marking Tadhg as your mate? He's requested for years to be allowed the chance to win you over, yet you will not even give him a moment of your time." He tapped the water sword on the floor. Waves appeared in the blade. "I don't comprehend why you won't let a man get close to you."

I sucked in oxygen from the winding and the pain of his words. Why consider choosing a mate because we'd hidden in the Summer Court for too long? The choices were slim and growing slimmer by the days. I wanted the longed for fated mate. Rarer than us Fae these days.

Not too many years ago, Mother and Father together sat down and told me and my siblings it was time for us to choose mates. To be happy. To produce more heirs to the throne and to show the Fae our lives in the Summer Court were still content. As royals, the Fae looked to us for everything. After all, his parents had forced Father to choose a mate when he turned two hundred years old. If not for destiny sending him Niamh that night, his true fated mate, he would have done as they commanded.

I charged the King with a mad swing and hit his sword time and time again. Each time I struck with my sword, a shudder ran down the length of my arm and into my shoulder. I needed to end this. I charged.

He elbowed me in the face. My head flung back as pain radiated from my cheek. The King dashed forward. I blocked his swing and punched his cheek. He staggered back. I lunged forward, blade extended for a finishing blow. He hit my stomach with the hilt of his sword.

Stupid. I heaved in breaths through the pain in my stomach. My knees wobbled as my vision blurred. Defeat loomed and I would need to subject myself to entertaining Tadhg. Tadhg wasn't a bad Fae, but he wasn't meant for me. *Shouldn't all of us have the chance to find our fated mates?*

Father found his fated mate. He had his queen by his side. *Was the time so long ago he didn't remember what it was like to look for a mate?* To want a true mate. Instead of settling with the one you didn't care for?

I gathered my last remaining conviction and raced across the floor, swinging with all the strength left in my arms and shoulders. Our swords thudded harder than any weapon forged by humans. With an almighty grunt, he swung at my middle and stopped short of cleaving me in two.

The quiet swish and green swirl of my sister Briana's gown caught the corner of my eye as she dashed into the room.

"Father," Briana said.

I kept my eyes on Father and matched him glare for glare, not daring to look away and show my defeat. His sword hung in the kill position. One wrong twitch, and he could end the sparring match with a final strike. But he'd never kill me. Sure, we'd injured each other in our sparring matches, but as Fae, we healed at an astonishing rate, and our Spring Baile healed more serious wounds.

"Briana, my child, what is it?" He narrowed his indigo eyes to slits.

"Something is wrong with Roisin."

His sword vanished in an instant as he drew his immense power back into himself, the sword and power an extension of himself. He straightened to face Briana. "What's wrong with my baby?"

Briana and I rolled our eyes. Roisin was fifty years old. Briana shrugged her shoulders in her elegant way. "She's asked to see you in her bedchambers. She won't get out of bed."

Father hurried across the floor, the thorns on his crown writhing with his anxiety over his child. He paused under the crystalline archway to turn and point a finger at me. "Tadhg will be here before long. You will at least meet with him."

I bowed my head. "Yes, Father."

I kept my head bowed so he wouldn't see the defiance in my eyes until his footfalls traveled across the marble floor of the great hallways.

"Tadhg's a talented lover," Briana said next to me.

I jerked to the side. "How do you always move so fast?"

"You could do worse than Tadhg." She ignored my question like she always did about her speed.

"If he was so talented, why didn't you choose him for your mate?"

She flinched like I'd struck her across the cheek. Briana had chosen a mate many years ago. A mate she'd been happy with. Who'd loved her. They'd had a child together. And she'd lost them both in the burnings.

"I'm sorry," I said, placing a hand on her shoulder. "This request of Mother's and Father's is hard on all of us."

"Aye." She sniffed. "Father has been more lenient with me, but I fear he'll recommence balls as a way for us to have a deadline."

"I never minded the balls. It might be fun to have them return to the Summer Court."

Briana scoffed. "So long as Father doesn't invite Tadhg?"

I scowled and curled my lip.

She half laughed as her fingers brushed over a flower in her princess crown. "I believe Tadhg has aspirations of marrying into the royal family."

"Aye." I ground my teeth. He'd moved on from attempting to win Briana over to me. "I'm tired of the endless bouquets he sends. How will I avoid him today?"

"I've helped you whenever I can, and today is one of those days. Hurry to the spring before Father returns." She flicked her long silver hair over her shoulder.

"What will you tell him when he finds out I'm missing?"

"The same story I tell him every time. You're a Fae princess, and as a Fae princess, we need to commune with our gift in solitude."

I laughed. "He believes you?"

Briana patted the long braid of her hair. "He has so far, but I don't think he believes you are looking for a mate. I've overheard other Fae men asking Father for permission to court you."

"Well, shite, no good can come of that."

"No."

I grabbed her hands. "Thank you."

"Perhaps you'll find the reason for the decline in the spring this time you secretly visit Earth."

I yanked my hands away from her soft grip. *Why did all my siblings believe I was the one to find the problem with the declining flow of the Spring Baile? Just because my power influenced water, it didn't mean I could solve this immense problem myself.*

"I hope so, too," I settled on saying.

A sharp whistle echoed across the courtyard. We jerked our heads in the noise's direction. Lorcan sauntered from under the crystalline arches, a giggling Fae woman on his arm. Trust my brother to break the tension with a Fae royal groupie. He had no problem looking for a mate, but choosing one wasn't something he intended to do in a hurry.

"Hey, girls, have you been fighting?" He ran his observant gaze over my bruised face.

I touched my aching cheekbone. "T'was Father."

Over the pain, a decadent warmth pooled low in my stomach, signaling my reproductive cycle was almost here. Not now, not when a Fae male was intending to court me. I'd never hold out against courting advances while in the clutches of a mind-numbing Fae heat, and if I allowed Tadhg into my bed while in heat, I'd end up pregnant and he'd assume I'd chose him as my mate. Father would encourage the mating. This would not do.

"I need to go," I said.

His nostrils flared. "You might want to hurry. I saw Tadhg heading toward the palace when I picked this one up." He nodded at the woman hanging on his arm with adoration blazing in her eyes.

"I'll tell Tadhg you're indisposed," Briana said.

I nodded my thanks. Briana might become annoyed about my power over water and my lack of finding the cause of our spring's decline, but she was a trustworthy sister. I kissed Lorcan on the cheek. He was my favorite brother, even with his promiscuous ways.

"I'll see you both later." With a glance at the royal groupie, I hoped our conversation was ambiguous enough that she didn't make anything of it.

I fled across the courtyard, under the crystalline columns, through the grand hallway of marble, and into the atrium housing the Spring Baile. The clear water trickled from the bright green moss-covered rocks and into the rock pool beneath. Once upon a time, centuries ago, the spring had gushed like a waterfall. Our precious water of life, abundant like the Fae. As the years churned, the spring slowed, and with each lessening trickle of the water, fewer babies were born to the Fae.

I splashed the water on my cheek. A tingle of healing power caressed my skin. I lifted my dress and touched a damp palm to my ribcage where Father had injured me in our sparring. It wasn't the first time, but today the match hadn't felt like a release of tension as he said, nor a lesson in learning how to sword fight. It was more a lesson in obedience. I'd never been the obedient child like my siblings.

The urgent surge of my impending heat spurred me into action. I touched a hand to the spring and summoned the Fae princess power I possessed. The veil between our world and Earth wavered but didn't allow me through as it had before Father placed the lock. But being family, our powers were similar. My brow furrowed as I twisted the lock and made a gap in the glittering veil to pass through. Being a Fae royal wasn't a bad thing when I could thwart my father's plans, bend the veil to my will, and walk on Earth amongst the humans. Use men without the consequences of pregnancy for humans couldn't impregnate a Fae.

The air shimmered with an indigo haze.

Freedom called to me.

I stepped through the veil onto Earth.

CHAPTER TWO
ARROW
AUSTRALIA

T HE LAST FIRE HAD taken its toll on me. Both in the flesh and the mind. Three weeks of fighting the fire from hell with the support of hundreds of ground and aerial firefighters. We all suffered the effects of this fire deep in our bones. The inferno of the Australian wildfire decimated almost half of Koala Island. 215,000 hectares burned. Homes and businesses destroyed. Farms and livestock lost. The fire reduced precious endangered wildlife even further. The worst was the loss of two human lives, a father and son trapped in a car together.

It hit too close to home. A cold lump in my heart that no matter how hard I believed losing them wasn't my fault, it wouldn't loosen the grip of its claws inside my chest. The wall of orange and red flames flashed in front of my face, along with the overpowering aroma of ash and cinders. Smoke. So much smoke. I scrubbed a hand across my bleary eyes.

Some years as a firefighter were tougher than others. This year started with the toughest fires so far, hot summer days and dry lightning strikes igniting blaze after blaze so close together they blurred into each other. But Australians were resilient. The community rallied around those affected, provided food and clothes, roofs to sleep under, water to drink, in a way that warmed every heart. The support of the people for its firefighters was bigger still. Some called us heroes. I didn't see it that way. I did what any able person would do in the circumstances, fought with my abilities to protect the innocent. We couldn't always protect nature from the destructive path of flames singing the white trunks and green leaves of eucalyptus trees, or the fern-like blue-green foliage of acacia shrubs. With time and rain, the blackened stumps and spindly bushes would flourish once more as nature reset itself.

I slicked back my hair, fiddled with my phone, then climbed out of my Ford Ranger and hauled in a breath of the ash-free night air of my hometown Crystal Creek. It was good to be home, safe, untarnished, except for the memories of the cloying smoke and the wall of flames that would keep me awake a bit longer yet.

The Pup's Tavern beckoned me like a friend, a building made of timber but full of warmth. And booze. I shoved my phone in my back pocket and waited for the rest of my team to arrive. We needed this night together to relax and unwind from our battle. To be home amongst the familiar setting of older buildings made from sandstone brick and tin roofs in the center of town and the outlying buildings made from timber as though a part of the forest. The surrounding eucalyptus trees stood silent like sentinels of all they surveyed and the wildlife living beneath their immense trunks. Their scent was soothing. A reminder of home. Underneath, the silver-gray branches of the acacias provided cover to the nocturnal animals whose yellow eyes I glimpsed from their depths.

The moon was full and high, shining on the silver paint of my Ford Ranger. It could do with a wash, but in the moonlight, it appeared unblemished. The tang of car fumes settled with the dust from my wheels, and an unusual scent drifted across the slight breeze of the summer's night. I lifted my head and scented the air. Heady and enticing, I curled my lip back and stepped away from my Ranger to follow the lure of the scent.

A massive Ford F-250 drove into the parking lot, hurling a brown cloud of dust over me and my pickup.

Sledge jumped out of his huge truck. "Dude, I almost ran you over."

"No shit."

"What were you doing in the middle of the parking lot, anyway?"

I rubbed a hand over my rough jaw, too busy to shave the last few days. I didn't know why I was standing in the middle of the parking lot. The scent was too sweet and enticing, too much like a secret I wanted to keep to myself. The settling dust destroyed the whiff of the scent I'd latched onto. An unerring certainty I was meant to follow the trail filled my mind.

Another Ford Ranger trundled around the bend and swerved in a more sedate manner than Sledge to avoid hitting us while we stood in the parking lot. The three remaining members of our team clambered out and slammed the doors.

"What are you two idiots doing?" Drago growled.

"Ask Arrow." Sledge shrugged his massive shoulders.

Drago eyed me. So did the twins, Lyle and Kirk, but I couldn't explain a scent I no longer smelled.

"First round is on me," I said and headed toward the front porch of the Pup's Tavern.

"Hell, yeah." Sledge slapped me on the back.

The others followed. As a team, we always followed and watched out for each other, even out of a fire. With each step, we progressed through the dust cloud, until I caught the scent again. I frowned, breathed deep. I ground to an abrupt halt. My black boots sent up more dust in the parking lot.

"Did anyone else catch the unusual scent?"

"Yep," Sledge said.

"What is it?" I asked.

"No freaking clue," Sledge said.

"That'd be a Fae." Drago rubbed the back of his neck.

"A Fae? Aren't they rare?" I asked.

"They are."

I drew in another breath. The scent made my mouth water. A Fae of all things in our little Australian wolf shifter country town, in the middle of nowhere. We lived far from humans, so they'd never discover our true identity. Humans had forced supernatural creatures into hiding many years ago. Long before my birth. I'd grown up hiding my wolf side from humans, as had the rest of my team apart from Drago, who was centuries old.

"What do you think they want?"

Drago inhaled. "Smells like one Fae to me."

"Yeah, I caught one scent," Sledge said. "What about you two?"

Lyle and Kirk nodded their heads.

"We've heard a rumor about a Fae visiting here," Lyle said.

"You don't say?" Drago frowned.

Lyle glanced away from Drago. So did Kirk. Even though they were fraternal twins, they exhibited the same mannerisms. The pair were an important part of our team with how easily they worked together, as though they read each other's minds and knew each other's movements.

"If a Fae visits Crystal Creek, why hasn't the rest of the pack learned about it?" I asked. More dust settled, and the scent grew stronger, more enthralling.

"It's a rumor," Kirk rushed to say.

I folded my arms over my chest. Lies. I scented Kirk's lie, but why lie about a Fae?

"Anyway," Drago said, "rumors aside, the scent I'm catching is female. I'm the oldest. I'll talk to her and see what she wants."

Female. Yes, the belief sent a rush of blood straight to my groin.

"No, I'm the captain of our team. I should be the one to question the Fae since no one else is at the tavern tonight," I said, noting the vacant parking lot except for our pickup trucks.

"They're all out on a hunt tonight," Sledge said. "Dad called me to see if I'd be back in time to join them."

"Convenient, you weren't."

Sledge shrugged. "Let's do our routine and pretend we don't realize what she is. It'll be the best way to find out what the Fae wants in Crystal Creek."

"You think she's here for nefarious reasons?"

"It'd piss Dad off if I didn't question another immortal's motives for visiting Crystal Creek and put the town's welfare first."

"And you don't want to be Alpha." I smirked.

"Shut up." Sledge headed to the door.

We caught up with him, each of us chuckling behind his back. This close to the source of the scent, it almost sent me to my knees. A rumbling growl filled my chest. My wolf raged inside me. Claim. Mark. Control. *Let me out.* I clenched and unclenched my fists. The sharp stab of my nails dug into my palms, producing clarity over the roaring need pulsing through every inch of my body.

The Fae scent was intense. Aromatic. Intoxicating.

I bit my lip. Blood welled to the surface. A metallic tang burst into my mouth, but it wasn't my blood my wolf wanted to taste.

My friend's gazes swung my way.

"Shit, Arrow, are you all right?" Sledge asked.

I growled.

They all stepped back in slow, measured movements.

I licked the blood from my lip and sealed the wound. I grasped the doorknob with a force that almost crumpled the round metal object in my palm.

"Arrow," Drago snapped. "Rein the change in."

I fought with everything I possessed to rein the throbbing need back to a dull ache and settle my wolf from his raging demands to let go and be wild.

"What?" I couldn't even form a proper sentence.

"Congratulations." Drago slapped my back. "You've found your mate."

"My mate?" I staggered back from the door. My wolf snapped at me to return to the door, to the alluring scent, to the woman omitting the aroma. "Are you saying the Fae is my mate?"

"Besides the Fae, I can scent Jim and Angus inside, unless one of them is your mate and you have told no one before now then...." Sledge chuckled and waved his hand at the tavern door.

Sledge boasted the best nose in town. If what he said was true, then... shit... the Fae was my mate. Every wolf shifter parent raised their offspring knowing there was one person fated for us. One whose scent would drive the beast inside us to claim them. Mark them as ours. Their scent alone was the sign. As was the special receptor inside us that gave us the awareness this person was our mate. We all waited for the day to arrive with excitement and anticipation. Wolf shifters revered mates above all else.

"I say we still go in with our plan," I said.

"Fine." Sledge flexed his fists. "Don't rip me to shreds."

"I won't."

Drago stepped back. "Arrow, once we get inside, you'll need to contain your wolf. He's going to go berserk. Your wolf won't like any other wolves or men near his mate."

"He already is. I can control him. We need to find out what the Fae wants, right?"

"Yeah, but not at the expense of us being attacked."

I huffed. "I won't attack you, any of you. For crying out loud, you make it sound like I'm a wild beast."

Drago chuckled. "Very well, oh civilized one, let's meet your mate and see if you can keep your shit together."

Lyle opened the door, and I growled. Sledge chuckled and slid in front of me, blocking my view of my mate. Kirk and Drago stepped around me and entered the door. I inhaled a deep breath to calm my wolf, which only drew my mate's scent in deeper and didn't soothe him at all. I followed them into the tavern.

The inside of the tavern was the same except for the aroma wafting over every inch of my skin, sinking deep into my pores and imprinting itself on my memory. I'd remember her scent for the rest of my life. One look at her and I'd memorize her face for eternity.

I placed a hand on Sledge's shoulder and met the indigo-rimmed eyes of my mate.

CHAPTER THREE
SAOIRSE

ONE MINUTE LONGER AND I wouldn't have made my way out of the Summer Court.

Whenever I passed through the Fae veil, my entry was over a lake, because of my power and affinity with water. Most places where I stepped through a forest encompassed the glassy lakes. Today had been no different. Gumtrees and scrub surrounded the large expanse of cerulean water for as far as my Fae vision could see—a land of wilderness. Pure instinct willed me to follow the small track to this tavern on the beaten dirt track.

I inhaled in relief inside the dusty interior of the outback tavern. Pickings were slim. One male bartender, too old and too flabby for what I required. The other male sitting on the barstool was too drunk even if he'd appealed, which he didn't in the slightest with his ass-crack hanging out of his jeans.

Damn my father for almost stopping my escape from The Summer Court. He could shove his choosing a mate idea up his rigid ass.

The moment I'd seen the tiny building with the bright orange veranda and timber decking, I'd known I wouldn't get what I required here. The building was the size of a large barn, resembled one too with the timber floor, and the leather circular bench seating filling the bar with the well-worn aroma.

Alcohol and leather mixed well together when you were looking for sex. It wouldn't be long, and I'd be in heat. The sensations were nothing new to me. I'd experienced them for centuries, and I'd found the way to combat the need was to give in to the heat.

But not with a Fae.

Before I fell in heat, I passed through the veil separating The Summer Court and Earth, lest a Fae man scent my heat and seek me out. Because the moment I was in heat, I became overcome with lust and carnal needs no one slaked until my heat was over.

And this time I'd almost slipped through too late.

I surveyed the two men with disgust. I should leave since neither of them were suitable to take for my lovers. A shudder of revulsion ran down my spine and settled in my stomach with sickness. I'd lowered myself during the first time of my escape in heat. Never again. Earth had changed since then. Showers and soap were pleasing inventions to the scent coming from humans. We Fae smelled identical to our power. Mine rippled with the scent of water, cool and sparkling. My power sat inside me, a glistening, fresh blueness.

I lifted my drink and downed the contents. I had no way to pay. Money didn't exist for Fae. In normal circumstances, I'd have selected a man to cover the alcohol and sex. I possessed neither money nor man, and I grew antsier by the second, but I could wait a few moments longer.

The door swung open, as if on cue, in walked five men. Five delicious, mouth-watering, thigh-clenching muscular men dressed in navy-blue uniforms. Their black booted feet echoed over the timber floor and through the empty bar. The men's deep male voices elicited a shiver over my back, washing away my earlier one of revulsion. Pickings weren't slim now. I sat up straight and stared at the men. *Which delicious male would satisfy me during my heat?*

They all appeared capable. Their shirt sleeves stretched tight around their biceps, thighs straining against blue pants and belt buckles taut, a sign of their virility. The man in front of the group caught sight of me and stopped in his tracks. His buddies attempted to shove by, but he held out his meaty arms.

"Dibs," the man in front growled.

He was large, broader than the rest, fists resembling sledgehammers, arms comparable to a wrestler, and legs similar to tree trunks. He could pick me up with one arm and carry me away with ease. I slid my gaze to his groin. In my experience, sizeable men akin to him weren't generously endowed, and I demanded generosity. The bigger, the better when my mindless heat overcame me.

The man behind him, dark and sexy, with golden eyes, snagged my gaze and held me captive. A flutter of exhilaration raced through my body. He placed a hand on the man's shoulder in front of him and leaned in to whisper in his ear. He was too quiet to overhear, and my hearing was out of this world. I frowned for a mere second, then smiled in invitation. Heat coiled low. I'd take either of the stunning specimens of men, so nigh to my heat.

The one who'd called 'dibs' stalked toward me while the others settled in a half-circle bench seat. The flicker of anticipation turned into disappointment that curled long and low as the golden-eyed man walked in a different direction, but he never took his gaze off me. I shifted my gaze to the man heading my way. His scent wafted over me, deep and dirty, filth and sex. He'd do. I smiled in welcome.

He placed a hand on the bar, the other on my lower back, and leered. "Baby, you're so hot you're on fire."

I stifled my snort at his tawdry pickup line and perused the badges on his uniform. Crystal Creek Fire Department on one bulging pectoral muscle, on the other 'Sledge'. Another snort sought to escape.

He leaned in closer. "I have a hose in my pants to help you put it out."

The snort escaped. Pickup lines were becoming worse over the centuries, not better. But I needed his 'hose' and I needed it soon.

"Sledge, leave the lady alone," said a dark and thrilling voice.

A hand landed on Sledge's shoulder again. I lifted my gaze to the golden-eyed man. He was breathtaking, dark, and dangerous, the way I liked my men. Thick eyebrows sat above his gold eyes, eyes that glittered with barely suppressed lust. A firm jaw peppered with dark black stubble surrounding sinful lips. He smirked, catching my stare, a flash of pointed white teeth. *With his mouth, would he be a biter?*

"But Arrow..." Sledge said.

"I said no." He growled deep.

A burning need scorched a trail over my nipples until they pebbled into hard peeks and jutted out through the lightness of my dress. This man—he was remarkable.

He drew in a deep breath, his nostrils flared, and his smirk grew.

Sledge walked over to his mates without a backward glance. Not an ounce of care entered my mind or body. My attention was on the soon-to-be sex Dia before me.

"Arrow." He held out his hand.

"Saoirse."

I placed my palm in his. He wrapped his fingers around mine. A warmth, unlike anything I'd ever experienced flowed from his skin to mine in a heated wave and progressed up my arm to caress the back of my neck.

"Unusual name." He swiped his tongue across his teeth. "Do you mind if I sit?"

I inclined my head toward the empty stool. "Does your ploy work with the ladies?"

I removed my hand from his grasp, and he sat next to me.

"What ploy?"

"The one where your friend comes onto me and you come to my 'rescue.'"

He chuckled. "Caught me."

"Is the rescue ploy because you're a firefighter?" I asked, taking in his matching uniform with the badge of the fire department and his name, Arrow.

"I enjoy rescuing a damsel in distress." His voice came out in a low, rumbling growl.

"I expect they're grateful and pliant."

He laughed. "Woman, you're something else."

"Look, Arrow." I ran my hand through my hair. One of my Fae princess flowers from my crown fell to the bar. Woman, Fae, he didn't need to comprehend what I was. I'd be on Earth a mere day while in heat.

His gaze tracked the motion, and he picked up the small white bloom, lifted the flower to his nose, and drew in a breath. "Yes, Saoirse?"

"I'm sure the ladies enjoy this 'getting to know you act,' but I don't give a shite."

His eyelids lowered, cutting the brilliant glare of his golden gaze. I placed a hand on his thigh and leaned toward him. The low cut of my floaty dress drew his gaze to my cleavage.

"We both know where this is heading. Let's cut the shite and get to gratification."

His eyebrows rose. His lust-filled gaze glittered and swirled with an intensity that'd have me on my knees begging if I wasn't sitting on a stool. I squeezed my fingers into the hard curves of his thigh.

He dropped his mouth to my ear and whispered, "Saoirse, I'd like to, but when I get down and dirty, I do it hard and harder still until you're screaming for me to stop and not stop at the same time."

Every inch of my body surged to life with lust and tingled from the tips of my ears to my little toe. I clenched my thighs, making it worse for the building need. I was so ready, and I wasn't even in heat yet.

"You like the sound of that, don't you?"

I nodded, causing the stubble on his luscious chin to scrape my cheek, eliciting a full-body shiver.

He shifted back. "First, I need to make sure you'll be okay with it, and I do that with this 'getting to know you crap,' as you so eloquently put it."

"One drink," I huffed.

"Three."

Oh, the man was determined. He'd pleasure with the same determination. I desired it. Desired all of him.

"Two," I countered.

I wouldn't last two, doubtful I'd last one, and for certain wouldn't last three unless they were shots and I slammed them. My heat loomed and the moment it arrived, I'd likely straddle him on the barstool to his cheering friends' delight. It wouldn't bother me. I was here for sex and only sex. In one day, I'd head back to The Summer Court, heat over, and no chance to fall pregnant, no Tadhg insisting I choose him as a mate. This one would be but another human male I'd used.

Arrow raised his index finger, and the flabby bartender rushed over. His stomach wobbled with each step. *Look at that, now he's eager to serve.* When I was alone, he'd been reluctant to approach me and serve me my paltry one drink, which had never been the way before. I shouldn't complain since I didn't have money. The male domination on Earth was shite, even more than in the Summer Court.

"What'll it be, Arrow?" the bartender asked his voice that of a man who'd smoked a pack of cigarettes a day since he'd been old enough to light one.

"The lady will have another, and I'll have a beer from the tap. Thanks, Angus."

"Back in a jiffy."

Arrow turned his attention to me. His gaze wandered across every inch of my face. I imagined he memorized what he saw. A dainty face with pale alabaster skin, wide crystal blue eyes resembling the power curled deep inside me. Long locks of gilded white hair hung in soft strands to my waist, dotted with flowers throughout the crown. My Fae princess crown.

"You're the most stunning creature I've met," he said.

Creature? Did he realize I wasn't human?

"You're a stunning creature yourself." I turned his words around on him.

He chuckled. "Honey, you have no idea."

"Neither do you." I baited him.

His eyes flashed, and his grin widened, showing his pointed canines. I'd never in my years seen teeth like his. They elicited a thrill of the unknown, of something wild and untamed. His navy-blue firefighter's uniform made him appear civilized, but beneath his burnished skin, he taunted and teased with restrained power.

"Touché. Let's move this forward, shall we?"

"Aye." I glanced at the door where outside and the freedom to ravage him without an audience beckoned.

"Uh-ah, not yet. Tell me about yourself."

I lifted a hand to my hair resting against my breast and brushed the strands back leisurely. The action never failed to draw men's attention to my physical assets. Arrow's gaze zeroed in on my fingers.

"Oh, I'm not so special." I lied. "Tell me about you."

Arrow's nostrils flared. His gaze shifted to mine, intense, and screamed 'liar' at me.

"I'm Captain of the Crystal Creek Fire Department." He drummed his fingers on the wooden bar top, tapping a tune. "I'm a local. I've lived here my entire life, and I'm positive you've never visited here."

"True," I said. "This is my first time in your delightful little town."

"Delightful? How much have you seen of the town?"

I waved my hand at the bar. "This."

"This bar? And you think it's delightful?"

"It's delightful compared to other bars I've frequented."

"Go to a lot of bars?" he asked.

"Some might say I do. It would depend on what you call a lot." I shrugged. After years of visiting the mortal realm, I'd visited plenty of bars hoping to find a man to help me during my heat. Some men scratched the itch, while others left the itch roaring like a disease. I hoped Arrow would put an end to the itch with his intensity.

"Twenty or more would be a lot."

"In that case, then aye, I've visited a lot of bars."

I brushed my hair over both my shoulders, revealing the hard tips of my nipples pressing against the soft material of my dress. His gaze dipped. He ran his tongue over his teeth like he imagined running his tongue over my nipples. I imagined it too.

"What do you do in the bars?" His voice dropped.

I shifted to the edge of the stool, closer to Arrow and the heat he generated along with the carnal scent of a pure untamed man.

"I pick up men."

A scratching sound on wood drifted up to me. I stared at his fingernails embedded in the timber bar. Small pieces of shredded wood littered the surface. *How did he scratch the bar?*

CHAPTER FOUR

SAOIRSE

"**A** RROW," THE BARTENDER RASPED in a warning.

I shifted back on the stool. The clink of glasses landed on the bar in front of us.

"Lady, it might be best if you leave." The bartender folded his arms across his chest.

"No," Arrow rumbled long and low.

"Get it together then."

A blur of movement in my peripheral vision showed the bartender walking to the other side of the bar, leaving me alone with Arrow. Every muscle in his body twitched. The wildness I sensed leashed beneath his exterior surged to the forefront for a brief second. With jerky movements, he lifted his hand and picked up his beer bottle. I followed the motion to his sinful mouth and the deep swallow of his throat, gulping the liquid. Heat rippled long and low through my stomach and along my thighs.

He placed the bottle on the bar and turned to me.

"Should I ask how many men?"

His voice elicited a warning of the rage simmering beneath the surface of his control. The idea of me with other men riled him. It sent a thrill through my insides and a jump to my heart. In my years with men, not one man displayed jealousy. No one cared about me. All they'd cared about was using me for sex, the way I used them.

Arrow was different.

I shifted my gaze away to my drink and lifted the glass to my lips for the first time with a quiver in my hand.

"No," I said into the still and quiet air of the tavern. "If my previous lovers make a difference to where this is heading, then I'll do as Angus said and leave."

"You won't leave," he commanded.

"I don't want to," I admitted, but I wouldn't be ashamed of the sex I'd endured to avoid the consequences back home in the Summer Court. "Should I ask how many women you've been with?"

"Six."

I raised my eyebrows. Such a small number, but he was human, and he didn't have my century's worth of years of combating a reproductive heat to contend with.

"So honest." I sipped my drink. It was refreshing, the drink and his honesty.

"I try to be. I'm not always successful." His sinful lips stretched into a grin.

I coughed to cover my laugh. "Nice to hear you have some faults."

"I have plenty, I can assure you."

"Name one?" I challenged.

"I love to eat peanut butter from the jar with a spoon."

"That's not a fault. That's a quirk and sweet."

"Sweet? No one has ever called me sweet before." He shook his head, sending his dark locks in a wave of movement.

The instant image of him standing naked, eating peanut butter from the jar swam in my mind. I picked up the glass and gulped the contents.

"That's one." I grinned. I needed to nudge this along faster. He intrigued me in a non-sexual way, too.

"So it is." He lifted his beer and drained the liquid.

His thick throat worked on deep pulls, and I envisioned his throat working as he suckled my nipple into his mouth. If they jutted out any further, they'd poke him in the eye. At least, then he'd be inclined to do something about them.

"Another of the same?"

"Whatever." Alcohol didn't affect me. I drank to appear human.

"What are you drinking?"

"Gin and tonic."

"I had you pegged for a vodka girl."

Girl? I hadn't been a girl for centuries. I stifled a laugh. In my bar-hopping sex trolling days, I'd drunk every type of alcohol imaginable over the years. Every drink tasted the same, a mixture of desperation and desire. Which is what I was right now.

He held up his finger to the bartender, signaling two more. His hands were gorgeous, like the rest of him.

Long and burnished. Nails trimmed short. *How did he scratch the bar?*

"Drink two is on its way. What should we talk about?"

"Sex." I exhaled. "What's your favorite position?"

He chuckled. "Doggy."

Should have guessed he'd like to take control. I almost felt him at my back, his heat draped over me as he nudged my entrance with his hard length. I shut my eyes and inhaled his scent. Dark male.

He placed a hand on the small of my back and shifted closer to me and whispered in my ear, "You like the sound of doggy, don't you?"

"Aye," I whispered back. "Let's do it now."

He shuffled back, and I snapped my eyes open to his golden ones. The bartender placed our second drink on the bar, two beer bottles.

"Drink number two first."

Damn him and his commanding tone. In secret, I loved it. I'd never partaken in this play before sex, never taken the time to get to appreciate my lovers before exhausting them. This was different. Arrow was different, and I longed for him more than I'd ever considered.

"Do you have any faults?" he asked. "Because from where I'm sitting, you're perfect."

"Perfect?" I scoffed. My father wouldn't call me perfect. I was the runaway princess, the one who wouldn't conform to the family's royal bidding to choose a mate and reproduce an heir. "Hardly."

"Why not? You're sassy, and I can tell you're smart. Sexy as hell, too."

"I'll take that as a compliment." I twirled the beer bottle in my hand.

"I meant it as one. What are you doing in my little neck of the woods?"

I peered at the window and the darkness outside. I couldn't see it, but the thick Australian forest sat outside the tavern. Tall gumtrees with silvery-brown bark reminiscent of ghosts in the fernery's greenness. Eerie and beautiful at the same time.

"I'm passing through for a few days." Not a lie, but not the truth, either.

His nostrils flared, but his gaze didn't flash 'liar'.

"Where are you headed?"

"Home." The truth. After my heat cycle, I'd head home.

"And where's home?"

"The other side of the lake." Not a lie either. He didn't comprehend I needed to step through the veil to return home.

"Ah." He placed a hand around his beer bottle and raised it to his lips. "I'm not getting any more out of you, am I?"

I shrugged. "You can get a lot out of me when we leave."

"Woman," he growled.

"Arrow." I smiled in a sultry, seductive way.

He shook his head but leaned closer. "You're something else."

"Something you want?" Without warning, a surge of uncertainty gathered at the bottom of my stomach. *What if he didn't want me? What if after the 'getting to know you' shite he didn't like me?* My brows puckered.

"Something I want badly," he rumbled in my ear. "So bad."

"I can be bad," I said against the side of his face.

He chuckled, moving back a fraction, somehow letting in the noises of his friends chatting across the other side of the room.

"You look too pretty to be bad."

I laughed. "Are you afraid you'll hurt me? Because I can guarantee I'll enjoy anything, I mean anything, you intend to do to me."

He swiveled on the barstool to face me with his legs splayed. I dropped my gaze to his groin, the enormous bulge in his pants evidence he desired me.

"Anything?" He lowered his voice and slid closer to me to capture me between his thick thighs.

I nodded. His heat and scent wafted to me, sending tingles over and through me. He ran his lips over my ear and caught the lobe in his teeth and bit down. I shivered.

"Even biting?" He released my lobe and grazed my neck with his teeth.

"Aye." I struggled not to moan.

"Hard enough to leave marks?"

"Aye." Oh, Dia, did I crave his mark on me, inside and out.

His hand landed on the curve of my waist, his fingers rubbed a tantalizing caressing back-and-forth motion over my eager flesh. "Pin you down and have my way with you?"

I'd never given sexual control to a man. I'd used them and taken what I required. Arrow was a man I wanted to experience.

"Aye." I slid my hand to the back of his head and said in his ear, "Anything."

I rubbed my cheek against his and rasped my sensitive skin over his spiky bristles. Dia, the sensation was wonderful. I craved for him to run his bristles along my body. Run him along my body. All of him.

He pulled back, and I almost fell from the stool.

"Two drinks first," he teased.

Damn him.

I lifted the bottle, finished the contents, and slammed it on the bar with a solid thud. The humans fell silent again. Heads turned our way, but my gaze was for Arrow alone. I rose from the stool and smoothed my dress in waves of softness. The long, silky fabric caressed my ankles. Underneath I was naked and slick moisture coated the insides of my thighs. The moisture wasn't from my impending heat. My need was for Arrow.

"Sit back down."

"No, I'm finished. You said two drinks. We consumed them. Now, either deliver on your word or I'll go over there..." I nodded toward the stunned audience. "And get Sledge or someone else to give me what I need."

"Like hell you will," he ground out, standing and shoving the stool backward, sending a screech across the timber floorboards.

"You can't tell me what I can and can't do." My power lunged for the surface with my anger.

He yanked me to him so fast I didn't see him move. His body hit mine in every delicious place. He smashed my aching breasts to his solid chest and ground my hard nipples across the roughness of his uniform's material. His bulging hardness pressed against my throbbing mound. But it was his mouth plundering mine, sweeping me up into a sea of desire which had nothing, absolutely nothing to do with my impending heat.

A sharp whistle drew Arrow's attention, and he lifted his head. Arrow threw a glance at the table, wrapped his large hand around my smaller one, the contrast in skin color obvious we were two unique creatures. Him a golden sun-tanned man, me an alabaster princess, but at this moment I longed to pretend I was human. To have him for me.

He dragged me across the bar to the door and shoved it open so hard the timber creaked. We strode outside. Where we were going, I didn't care, so long as I had him soon, buried deep, surrounding me with him, his scent, his heat, his hardness.

We made the distance across the parking lot to the edge of the forest before he spun me around, brushed the hair from the nape of my neck, and wrapped his lips around the coolness of my flesh. He drew my skin into his mouth and suckled. My knees wobbled, and I crumpled to the ground to kneel with him behind me. He tugged on both my nipples with his firm fingers until they burned with pleasure.

"More," I begged.

Arrow chuckled against my neck and dragged one hand to my back and ran his palm along my spine. He scrunched the long material of my dress up to my waist while his other hand toyed with my nipple. Every tug and twist shot need to my clenching core.

"No underwear." He breathed against the sensitive skin on the back of my neck. "Naughty girl."

He rubbed his hand over the cheeks, then smacked them with the firmness of his palm.

"Take me," I moaned, dropping to my hands and knees, and offering myself up to him in his favorite position.

"That's the plan." He chuckled and dipped his fingers to my slick entrance. "So wet."

Whatever words I'd held on my tongue for a comeback disappeared. He ran his fingers along my folds and over my clit. My hips bucked, and I strained back into his hand, impatient for more. He obliged with a slow slide of his finger. I shuddered. Every muscle in my body quivered in response to his intense heat. He dipped and swirled over and over, commanding me closer to the edge, and I wasn't in heat yet.

I panted into the darkness of the forest, and the sounds of the night creatures wandering amongst the foliage. It didn't matter they were our audience. What mattered was Arrow and what he did to my body.

He slid his fingers out and over my puckered entrance. I dug my hands into the gritty earth.

"I wanted this to last," he growled. "But next time."

His disappearing fingers left me bereft. The warm summer night air drifted to my damp folds. His zipper rasped in a wrench of metal teeth. Then his hands landed on my hips and the bunched material of my dress. His rigid cock teased my opening. He drew me back and slammed into me, hard. Every nerve ending inside me ignited in ecstasy as his length filled me in a way no man or Fae ever had. My muscles tightened on him, never wanting him to leave as his flared head rubbed the spot deep inside that sent me soaring into the realm of release.

"Aye," I cried, my muscles clamping on his firm length and exploding into a rippling orgasm. *What was that?* I hung my head and gave myself over to the unexpected pleasure undulating through my body.

"You feel amazing." Arrow groaned.

He held my hips to his groin. Buried himself deep as though he didn't want to leave my heat either. Didn't want to end this instant pleasure. I bucked and wreathed against him as my orgasm jerked my body with a force he'd managed from one thrust and one thrust alone.

"I want you to come for me again."

"Arrow…"

"That's it, honey, say my name. Know who's fucking you tonight."

"Do it then," I complained when he still hadn't moved, and my orgasm ended.

"Oh, I will." He drew back and slammed into me.

Thank you, Dia. He didn't hold back. He pounded into my willing flesh, still sensitive from my earlier orgasm, but more. My heat was here, and the intensity hit me with the force of a blinding crescent. Arrow paused, balls deep. He inhaled, long-drawn-out.

The skin on his arms quivered so intensely, it seemed almost as though it rippled and pulsed. A soft silkiness against my neck replaced his stubbled chin. I attempted to turn my head, but his mouth latched onto the base of my neck and shoulder. His teeth dug in with a blinding sting of pain and pleasure. He moved then, pinning me in place with his body and teeth while his cock surged in a brutal rhythm.

My power burst free, bringing a light mist to descend upon us, responding to whatever Arrow did to me. I sobbed with the pleasure and gave myself over to Arrow, surrendering in entirety. Over and over, in and around me, he surrounded me with his presence, coated me with his scent, his very essence.

His finger sought my clit. One brush, then two, and I exploded with blinding stars behind my eyelids and a roaring howl in my ears.

Or was the sound Arrow's roar of pleasure?

He exploded with me, the powerful surge of his length pulsing in time against my clenching walls, turning the world to bliss and pleasure and everything that was him.

CHAPTER FIVE
ARROW

S AOIRSE'S BODY DRAGGED MINE to the pinnacle of pleasure and beyond. Her tight sheath surrounded my pulsing dick with a rightness that blew my mind. Sex never had so much meaning than with my mate. I wanted more of it. More of her.

My vision hazed with the pleasure and the misting rain surrounding us, but then everything was a hazy blur of want and need from the moment I caught sight of the Fae woman, my mate, perched on a stool in my hometown tavern. I'd believed her scent alluring, but the picture of her beauty held me captive and right now, bent over and accepting me from behind, she was the most beautiful sight to behold. I could stare at her beauty all day and night. To see me taking her in every position possible.

I ran my hand up her back, sending another shiver down her spine. When Sledge had placed his hand on her back, I'd wanted to rip his arm from his body and beat my best friend with his bloody stump.

So, this was what having a mate felt like.

I circled the bite mark on her neck with a finger. Her sheath clenched around my semi-hard dick. If I stayed like this, I'd lose my mind and ravish her on the floor of the forest again. Keeping my shit together around my mate was harder than I'd ever imagined. I'd attempted to question her, but those questions didn't matter. She was my mate. Nothing mattered but her. My dick boasted a mind of its own and swelled inside her. My wolf wanted to growl and howl with pleasure at the same time.

I willed myself not to pound into her welcoming heat again. Saoirse. Her name murmured through my mind and made my heart pound at the beauty of her. I'd spend the rest of my life whispering her name in reverence. She blinded me to everything except her.

And her sassy mouth...

I wanted to capture her lips with mine again, and experience her sass against my lips, hear her moan my name again. My wolf rumbled in satisfaction. I lapped at the mark and the tiny droplets of blood on the back of her neck. She squirmed under my touch. *Did she feel the mark as profoundly as I?*

I willed the urge to bite her again to wait until I entertained her in my home. How I'd lasted two drinks before dragging her outside to claim for my mate was anyone's guess but claim her I had. Her heat and slickness surrounded me, welcomed me, and I didn't want to budge. I didn't want to leave this idyllic place of being one with my mate.

I'd marked her as my mate, buried my teeth into the soft flesh of her neck with the rightness of the moment. Even if I'd wanted to, I couldn't have stopped myself. My wolf urged me to mark her. Claim her. Show the world she was mine. I wasn't sure what would happen next since she was a Fae. So different to me. But mine all the same.

I'd make this mating work.

It wasn't like either of us had a choice now.

A mating was for life. If I'd been thinking clearly, I would have asked her permission first, as was the way with wolf shifters. It shouldn't have even been possible to mark her. A wolf's mating mark only worked when it was accepted. Normally discussed beforehand in a civil way. What happened between us had been pure instinct.

I had to win over the woman. Fae. I still didn't quite believe a Fae was in our town to begin with, but I was grateful I'd found my mate.

Found her. Marked her. Now I'd keep her.

CHAPTER SIX
SAOIRSE

"**F**UCK ME," ARROW GROWLED, his desirable body draped over mine.

"Just," I gasped, "did."

He slid out of my body, his length hard again, and hauled me to my feet in a smooth, quick motion. *How strong is he?* His zip wrenched up, a metallic sound in the quiet of nature. He spun me around, tugged me to his chest, and wrapped his arms around me. I inhaled his delicious sex scent through his uniform.

"I didn't mean to do that," he mumbled, his breath rustling my hair.

"Not complaining." I sighed.

His thumb brushed my neck where he'd bitten. A sensitive tingle drifted from the unexpected tenderness and wrapped around my heart.

"Why is it raining?" he asked.

I sighed again, so lost in him and his warmth I didn't care my power still showered us in the light, misting rain.

"It's the hottest summer on record and we have rain?"

"Sorry," I said so low he wouldn't catch it. I lifted my hands behind his back and called my power inside with a monumental effort. My power sought to stay free, to linger in the night's pleasure like I desired to do with Arrow.

"I love the smell of rain." His chest expanded beneath my face. "But we should get out of here. Come home with me?"

I nodded my head, brushing my face and hair against the stiff material of his uniform.

"Where's your car?"

"I don't have one."

"Bags?"

"None."

"What the? How the?" He shifted me back to peer at my face. "I thought you said you were passing through on your way home?"

"I am."

In the darkness under the foliage of the forest, his golden eyes narrowed, screaming his liar accusation at me yet again.

"How did you get here, then?"

"Walked." The truth too. I'd walked from the lake.

"Come. I'll take you home in my pickup."

He slipped his hand into my mine and tugged me toward a row of vehicles. We paused at a shiny silver vehicle. He released my hand to fish in his pocket for the keys, unlocked the truck, and opened the car door for me. Such a gallant gesture, and I stifled a laugh after the way he'd taken me on the ground, hard and dirty as he'd promised. Arrow shut the door and circled the vehicle to the driver's side.

The engine purred to life, vibrating through the leather seats and igniting my need again. He slammed the car in reverse and sped out of the parking lot and along the dark dirt road through the gum trees. Arrow threw me sideways glances every few minutes. The tension between us skyrocketed. *What was his problem?*

"You don't have to take me home if you don't want to."

He jerked in the seat. "I want to."

"What's your problem?" If he was honest, he'd tell me. "I didn't hurt you, did I?"

"No," I scoffed. "I said you wouldn't."

"I don't understand what overcame me back there." He shook his head. The dash lights lit up his confused expression.

"Sex." I couldn't very well tell him the pheromones from my heat affected him and drove him wild. "You won't hold back when we get to your place, will you?"

"Hold back?" His voice choked in a strangled pitch. "Honey, I'm having a hard time holding back now. When I get you to someplace with more room, I'll devour your sweet body all night. One taste wasn't enough."

I smiled in anticipation as my insides pounded with need. "How much farther?"

"Not far."

He swung the pickup around a bend at breakneck speed for the dark dirt road. The least of my worries.

I was immortal. But I didn't wish for Arrow to die. The notion sent a clench of panic to my heart. *What was this sensation?*

I ignored the reaction and concentrated on the heat and lust filling the cab. The air grew thick and his eyes glowed gold in the darkness. Every few breaths, he'd inhale deep, a flare of his nostrils and surge of his chest.

I eyed his lap. The need to straddle him while he was driving coursed through me. He'd handle it, but I craved to experience more of his dominance and control. For once, I sought a man to take care of my needs instead of me using him to satisfy my needs. I shut my eyes.

What was so different about Arrow?

The car jerked to a stop, and I snapped my eyes open. In the gleam of the headlights sat a concealed timber cabin nestled in the forest, resembling a piece of nature. His home appeared undomesticated in the same way he was untamed and wild. I opened the door and stepped out. My power surged to the surface with the sentiment of coming home. I gasped at the unexpected impression. The Summer Court was my home. A light, misting rain descended on my face and coated my eyelashes. My power agreed with my feelings.

"What is with this rain?" Arrow asked.

I shrugged, opened my palms to the sky, and lured my power inside, stopping the rain with the same abruptness as I'd called the water to fall.

Arrow ran an assessing gaze over me.

"Are you pleasuring me outside again or inside?" I asked to deflect him. He was too astute with his golden gaze.

He inclined his head, eyes growing hooded. "Come here and find out."

I walked around the hood of the vehicle, a sway to my hips meant to entice him further the way I'd always performed with other human men. His sexy smirk and knowing gaze drew me and showed me he desired me with every part of him. My enticement wasn't necessary with him. The lust I experienced for Arrow was more than my heat, threads of feelings tugged at my heart, and my power hummed in approval. I stopped in front of him, unsure if I was doing the right thing by using him.

His enormous hands wrapped around my waist and hoisted me onto the hood of his car. My butt landed on the warmth of the damp metal and I squeaked with surprise. He grinned and licked his teeth. I longed for his hot and possessive bite again. To experience his teeth nudging into my flesh, the rasp of his tongue as he sucked my flesh into his mouth, and the feelings of rightness that happened with it. A desire so strong rippled through my body and settled in my stomach.

He leaned into me and ran his tongue along my lips. My mouth parted, eager for his kiss, but he jerked back and urged me to lie on the hood. He wrapped his fingers around my ankles and tugged my body to the edge of the car. His hands slipped under my dress, dragging the material higher and higher with his wandering fingers.

I stared at the night sky. Darkness surrounded but for the slight glow of yellow light at the front door and the pale whiteness of the moon shining over the branches of the trees, casting shadows of seduction.

His lips landed on the inside of my thigh and he sucked the skin into his mouth before sinking in his teeth. I writhed beneath him. His hands pinned my hips. His mouth released my willing flesh, and his tongue rasped a long lick over my slick folds.

"Oh, pleasure me, again," I gasped.

"I intend to," he mumbled into my aching flesh.

He resumed the caress of his tongue on my clit, tiny quick licks making me spiral toward orgasm in a matter of minutes. My thighs trembled. My back bowed from the heated metal. His hands held me still to his ministrations. He was in control of my body and I loved he was the one demanding my pleasure.

He thrust his tongue inside. I pulsed with release while he lapped and licked at my trembling flesh in ways I'd never experienced. He rose above my still-quivering flesh, unzipped his pants, and thrust into my heat. Lust swirled higher and hotter. I lifted my hands to his chest, frustration filled me when they met material. I yearned for him to be naked. I fumbled with the buttons. He grabbed my wrists and pinned them over my head with one of his large hands.

Arrow pumped into my greedy flesh deliberately slow. I wrapped my legs around his waist and dug my heels into his tight ass cheeks, urging him to go faster and harder.

"Uh-ah," he said. "This time I want it to last."

Last? I was already almost there again. My breath fell in shallow pants. His broad head brushed along my clenching walls, hitting the sensitive spot deep inside with blinding clarity. I shut my eyes and my vision faded to nothing.

"Keep them open," he growled.

I snapped my eyes open at his command. I relished it. Adored him inside me. Over me. Through me. *What is he doing to me?*

"Arrow," I moaned. "I want you naked."

He chuckled. "I want you naked, too. Next time."

Aye, next time. I stared into his eyes. They burned in extremeness. If I'd been human, they would have hurt. I gave myself over to Arrow. Wave after wave of his slow carnality crested to the top and then I fell over the edge.

"That's it, honey. Watch me as you come."

His words, his presence, his everything commanded me. I gasped, then screamed. My orgasm peaked on his slow pumps in and out over my quivering flesh. His hips bucked under my heels and he buried himself to the hilt, threw back his head, and howled to the moon and the night sky.

The hairs on my body stood on end, but I couldn't tear my gaze away from the spectacular creature pulsing inside me.

Creature?

Shite, is he not human?

CHAPTER SEVEN
SAOIRSE

T HE WARM METAL UNDER my backside cooled in an instant, or perhaps it was me. I pushed my hands against Arrow's firm chest and unhooked my ankles from his waist.

"Arrow," I said with trepidation.

He tilted his head, a predator's gleam to his smile. His pointed teeth flashed white under the glow of the moon. Then he blinked, and the smile disappeared. He was Arrow, a glorious specimen of a man.

"Did I hurt you?" He frowned.

"No, of course not," I scoffed.

"Good." He hauled me up by my hands and urged me against his chest.

A peculiar comfort after my moment of uncertainty he wasn't human. Of course, he was human. *What else could he be?* I sensed no magic or powers emanating from him.

"I did it again, didn't I?"

"Did what?" The trepidation was back.

He scrubbed a hand through his hair, and I lifted my head.

"I'm sorry. Should've used a condom. I'm clean, but... there's always the chance of pregnancy."

He seemed so distressed. I placed my palm on his rough cheek.

"It's all right. I'm clean too and I can't get pregnant."

True, Fae didn't catch human diseases, and mortals couldn't impregnate immortals. So, everything was fine.

"Thank fuck for that." He exhaled. "You're something else. I keep losing my mind with you and your scent, your flavor, everything."

"My what?"

"You. You're like the first spring rain, and I love the rain."

"You're sweet, aren't you?"

I placed my other hand on his cheek and drew his face to mine. We kissed in a tender exploration of lips. My heart thudded. *What was he doing to me?* I broke the kiss.

"Are we sitting outside all night, or going inside?" I asked.

He withdrew his semi-hard cock and zipped up his pants. *Would I ever see him naked?* He scooped me into his arms and carried me toward the front door.

"I can walk," I squeaked.

He hauled me tighter into his arms. "I'm not letting you go."

"What?"

"You're mine."

"Arrow..."

His lips landed on mine, hard and demanding. He thrust his tongue into my startled gasp and coaxed me back to a new panting high. He stopped kissing me long enough to unlock the door and carry me over the threshold. Once inside, he lowered me to my feet.

"Welcome home," Arrow said.

My palms grew damp, my power surged beneath my skin. I couldn't release my power inside his house. But his words affected me. Mine. Home. The worst part, I sensed they were true in the very depths of my being.

I spun away from him and his masculine allure. He was just a man to use. Nothing more. He flipped on the light switch, illuminating a wide-open room. A deep blue modular sofa lined the wall and a gigantic window dotted with the rapidly drying raindrops from my power looked out into the dark forest. The place felt so him. Deep, dark, male.

He stalked toward me. His booted feet were quiet on the carpeted floor, but I sensed him as though we were two halves now joined. He caressed his fingers through my hair, sending a shiver along my spine.

"Would you like a drink?"

I shook my head.

"Something to eat?"

I shook my head again.

"What do you want?"

I turned toward him. "You. Naked."

"I want you naked too," he said, his voice rumbling. He dropped his head and kissed the side of my neck with a delightful trail of his lips. "But first I need food."

"Food?"

"Yes, I'm hungry. Our squad got back from Koala Island today. Damned wildfires ravaged half of it."

He was a damn hero, and I was ruining him. I stepped back out of his reach.

"Would you like a towel or a change of clothes?" he asked.

"No, why?"

He ran his gaze over my body. My skin tingled as though he'd run his fingers over me.

"Your dress is damp and see-through."

I dropped my gaze. Sure enough, the pale pink dress was transparent, showing my dark rosy nipples in their eagerness.

"I'm fine." I shrugged.

"You're not cold?"

"I don't feel the cold and it's not cold in here."

"Huh? Yeah, it's been a long, hot summer around these parts. Come with me to the kitchen."

He wrapped his warm hand around mine and tugged me toward his kitchen. The pale gray carpeted flooring gave way to stone gray tiles. Timber and stone made the kitchen. Oak timber cupboards, a shiny granite bench top, and the oven surrounded by brickwork, all of it masculine, like Arrow.

I tugged out a stool and sat at the bench while he opened the fridge.

"How long were you away?"

"Two weeks."

He shut the door and held a blood-red package.

"My mom fills the team members' fridges for our return. Are you sure you don't want a steak?" He eyed the size of the package with hunger.

"I don't eat meat."

"What." He staggered back and planted a hand on his stomach. "Woman, what have I got myself into?"

I shrugged and picked up a glossy red apple from the fruit bowl in the middle of the bench and tossed it up in the air. The apple slapped my palm on its return. He didn't need to worry. I wouldn't be here long. The notion sent pain slicing into my chest and throbbing to my neck. I lifted a hand and touched my neck, but I found nothing wrong under my fingers.

His gaze followed the motion, his brows puckered, and he scrubbed a hand over his jaw.

"I should..."

"You should what?"

"Cook this steak," he said briskly.

He turned to the stove and removed a pan from the cupboard next to it. He worked with confidence in the kitchen, at ease in an understated masculine way.

"You might at least do this naked and give me entertainment while I'm waiting."

He chuckled. "I thought *I* was insatiable. There's no way I'm cooking on a hot cooktop naked. Nope. Too much chance to get burned."

I pouted. "I'd kiss you better."

"As tempting as your offer is..."

Heat and lust simmered in his gaze, raking my body to settle on my breasts. My nipples drew tight, and he passed his tongue over his teeth. He turned to the cooker and set the steak in the frypan. Then he chopped vegetables and set them in another pan with herbs and butter, filling the room with delicious aromas. My mouth watered with the fragrance of food.

Every few minutes he'd throw me a look or a smile while he worked, keeping me aware he hadn't forgotten me in his home. I swiveled on the stool and examined his house. There wasn't one ounce of femininity in the place. No flowers or plants, no paintings hanging on the walls, or throw cushions on the sofa. Even without those things, a sense of peace seeped through the place and found its way to me. I swung my head and swiveled back to Arrow.

Everything was different with him.

Men's houses were places to sate my needs. Not a place to experience emotions. No, not while I was in heat. It was about sex and orgasms. Lots of them too. For the moment, Arrow had sated the wave of my heat and it now simmered at a comfortable level. Strange, more often than not, I'd be prowling, ready for more while the man recouped for another round. I didn't believe Arrow required the recouping time, but he demanded it. Similar to how he'd demanded my pleasure.

I longed for more of his control, just as strongly as I longed for more of him.

He plated his steak and dished the vegetable medley on two plates, then carried them over to the counter and placed one in front of me.

"You cooked for me?" I gulped.

"I know you said you weren't hungry, but I don't enjoy eating alone."

Raw vulnerability. Mine and his. No man ever cooked me a vegetarian dish. Ever. All they'd ever desired was sex. Sex was what I was good at. This was new. Scary. Fragile. Tears simmered.

Arrow stalked to the other side of the kitchen and returned with flatware and two glasses of sparkling crystal-clear water. I picked up the glass and sipped the power into me, hoping the soothing water would calm these damn tears threatening to spill over my lashes.

I cleared my throat. "Thank you."

"You're welcome, Saoirse." He brushed a hand along my back.

A unique tingle raced over my skin that had nothing to do with my heat. Which was no longer pressing upon me with urgency now I was in Arrow's house. Before I examined what transpired between us, I raised my fork. I didn't need this. I only required sex. Sex, identical to the sex we'd already enjoyed. But naked. Aye, I intended to see every inch of his burnished skin.

He cut into the thick steak, and red blood oozed from the pink-seared flesh. I wrinkled my nose. *Why did humans insist on eating flesh?* He placed the steak in his mouth and winked at me. Damn him, he was too much.

"What's your last name, Saoirse?"

"Smythe." I stabbed a chunk of the orange vegetable. Pumpkin, I assumed.

He chuckled. "Couldn't come up with a better fake surname?"

"Fake? What makes you think it's fake?" I spluttered.

"I have a nose for lies." He tapped the side of his nose. I'd wondered...

"Doesn't matter." He shrugged.

"What doesn't matter?"

"Your lies. You'll tell me your secrets soon."

"Is that right?" I waved the fork in the air. "What makes you so sure?"

"Because you want me, and you want me to appreciate you."

"I... what..." I coughed.

"Don't worry, honey." He met my gaze with a deep intensity of emotions swirling in his eyes and said, "I feel it, too."

I shoved the fork in my mouth, an explosion of flavors burst over my tongue and coated the back of my mouth.

"This is amazing." I stabbed another piece and ate more.

"My last name is Goldstein, in case you wanted to know."

He ate more of his steak. Dia, I wanted to know. *Why? Why him?* The skin on the back of my neck heated. I touched a hand to the place burning my body. My skin wasn't warm to my probing fingers. Arrow reached across and caressed the back of my neck for a minute, then resumed eating his steak.

"Do you have a family?" he asked around a mouthful.

"Aye, they're back home."

"Brothers? Sisters?" He paused and eyed me.

I sighed. He was determined to be acquainted with me. *What harm would there be to tell him a little about me?*

"Two brothers, four sisters."

"An extensive family. What are their names?" He resumed eating.

"Rian, Briana, Aislinn, Lorcan, Ciara, and Roisin."

"Unusual names like yours."

I'd lived so long in the Summer Court I had no real concept our names were no longer familiar on Earth.

"Our family originated from Ireland. We keep the tradition with the Irish names," I said.

His eyebrow rose. "Are you close?"

"I'm closest to Lorcan. We're close in age, the total opposites, but we get along." The power he'd chosen to hone were the complete opposites, mine was water, and Lorcan's was fire, but for all our opposite powers, he was the one sibling I connected with the most.

"That's good you're close. And where are you in there? Oldest? Youngest?"

"I'm in the middle."

"Piggy in the middle, huh?"

"You could say that. More akin to the forgotten one unless they want something from me."

"What do they want from you?"

I heaved a deep breath, drawing in his scent. Dark, male filled my senses, grounding me to the here and now. To sex and lust of my heat, but more to the longing buried beneath the surface deep inside my heart for a man to call my mate.

"They want me to listen to my father's demands." I placed my fork on the counter, surprised to find my plate empty, and more surprised I'd told him about my father.

"What does your father demand of you?"

"He preaches about family responsibility." I brushed back the loose strands of my hair. "Do you have a family?"

He tugged my stool closer to his and threaded his fingers through my hair. Every place I touched, he sought to leave his mark on me.

"Only my mom now." Sadness tainted his expression.

"What happened?"

What was wrong with me? Why was I asking him questions?

"My two older brothers and father died in a wildfire. A tree fell on their fire truck and flames overwhelmed the vehicle. The damage trapped them inside."

"Oh." I placed a hand on my mouth. Images of my family burned on the stakes surfaced in my mind. I understood his pain. "I'm so sorry, Arrow."

"It's okay, honey, there's nothing anyone could do. They were heroes. They saved the town, but..."

I slid from the stool and wrapped my arms around him. He hugged his arms around my waist and buried his face in my hair. An unfamiliar sensation filled me. Not associated with my heat, or lust, or the need for sex. A desire for a connection with this stunning man slammed into my chest.

I tilted my head to the side and kissed his unshaven cheek. He turned to kiss me.

I wrenched my head back. "Ew, your breath smells of meat."

He chuckled. "I'll brush my teeth. How about a shower, too?"

He flashed his pointed white teeth. Lust barreled to the surface.

At last, I'd have him naked.

CHAPTER EIGHT
ARROW

I HAD MY MATE in my home, filling me with a sense of wonder and warmth. She was even more beautiful inside my house, sitting on my stool and eating my food. I wanted to feed her for the rest of my life. Look after her and care for her in any way she needed. Her warm, enticing scent forced a roaring need to my dick, ready to give her what she needed.

I shifted away from her and filled the sink with water. She sauntered over and stood next to me.

"I thought we were showering?" She ran a hand up my arm.

"Soon. I'll clean up in here first."

Her touch was making my wolf rumble. I wanted to change and show her my soft fur, have her run her fingers along my back, and scratch under my chin. Let me free to be wild.

"So domestic."

I chuckled. If only I could show her the wildness of my wolf. She'd never call me domestic again. "No one else is here to do it."

"No girlfriend?"

I scrubbed a plate, then met her gaze. "You think I'd bring you home if I had a girlfriend?"

My wolf snapped. There'd be no other woman now we had our mate.

"I barely know you." She shrugged. "Who knows what you are like? I've been with men who failed to mention they had a girlfriend or wife."

"I'm not like that. There's no girlfriend. No woman here besides you."

There wouldn't be a woman here besides her. She was it. The one woman meant for me. The one meant for my wolf, too.

She slid her hand down my arm and picked up the checkered tea towel. "How does a man like you not have a girlfriend?"

I handed her a clean plate. "I guess you haven't seen the size of the town?"

"No. T'was night when I arrived."

"That's right, you arrived without a car, no luggage, and in the dark." I washed another plate.

She said nothing.

I sighed. *Why wouldn't she tell me more about herself? If I told her about me, would she open up? Or would she run?* I wanted to pace instead of wash dishes. I scrubbed the pan harder than necessary. Saoirse waited in silence. I handed her the clean pan. Her fingers brushed mine in a soothing caress. I settled and so did my wolf, from the barest of touches from our mate.

"Anyway, there aren't many people in this town. Meaning there aren't many women to have as a girlfriend, and other women find this town too small."

"It's a wonder the people stay in the town." She placed the pan on the counter and held her hand out for the next clean dish to dry.

I scrubbed the saucepan with less vigor and handed her the clean item. "Us townies love Crystal Creek, its seclusion, the peace, the forest, and the lake and waterways are spectacular."

Not to mention the witches had cast a protection spell around the town to keep our existence a secret.

"I saw the lake. The water was picturesque with the moon glinting off the gentle ripples."

"I love the water. We should swim tomorrow."

"I'd like that." Her blue eyes glistened like deep pools of water themselves.

I grinned and contained my small internal high five of triumph. I needed to prove to Saoirse she belonged here, with me, and it needed to be more than sex. As good as the sex was between us. A hard knot of guilt settled in my stomach. I should talk to her. Should've talked to her before we'd left the bar. I scrubbed the flatware and handed them to my mate. I wanted to call her my mate out loud and yell it from the treetops. Declare our mateship to the townspeople. Hug my mom when I told her. She'd be so happy I'd found my mate. Although...

No, I shook the reflection off. It'd been so long since most of the Fae left the Earth. Surely everyone was over their desertion by now.

"You like to tease, don't you?"

I laughed.

"Honey, I like to tease you, and you love it when I do."

She huffed, but her cheeks turned a pretty shade of pink.

"You love it when I run a teasing finger over your hand."

I did the very thing I said, wiping my damp finger over the back of her hand. A ripple of goosebumps exploded up her arm.

"Your touch is pleasant."

"Pleasant?" I quirked an eyebrow. "What about when I touched your wet pussy? Was that pleasant?"

She licked her bottom lip with a quick swipe of her pink tongue. I almost groaned at the quick flick I imagined over the tip of my dick.

"Aye," she said, her voice husky.

I washed a glass, watching the suds fill the inside. Deep inside, my wolf settled in a calm stretch of rightness with Saoirse by our side. I imagined this for our life, eating side by side, clearing the dishes side by side, walking to the bedroom together, and filling our nights with long caresses. Scratch that, filling our days with passionate kisses and caresses, too.

Fuck, I wanted her again so badly my body ached with need.

Easing closer to her, I ran my lips over the soft skin below her ear. She trembled beneath my exploring lips.

"What about when I kiss your neck? Is that pleasant too?" I eased back from her.

Her body swayed, chasing me in my retreat.

"Aye." She dipped her head, making the long length of her white-blonde hair cascade over her chest.

"And when I lick your clit?"

She moaned.

After shoving the glass into her hand, I washed the last item. I'd dragged this out long enough. I was rock hard. My aim was to get to know Saoirse more and entice the woman to want me for more than sex, but it was impossible with her enticing scent. I yanked the plug and dried my hands on the tea towel in Saoirse's hands.

I wanted her for sex, and so much more.

CHAPTER NINE
SAOIRSE

MY SKIN TINGLED IN anticipation of Arrow's electrifying touch again as though every inch of my body longed to be plastered against him. To be kissed and licked. Held and caressed. Blood roared through my body. My power rose. Whatever happened between Arrow and me, my power responded on its own.

He wrapped his large hand around mine and led me through the hallway toward his bedroom. We passed his gigantic bed, and I imagined us in it. A timber frame set high off the ground and covered in a deep burgundy cover. In front of the bed sat an open fireplace and a fluffy black rug. I wanted to sink on the rug and run my hands over the black strands to find out if the fur was as soft as it appeared. On the other side of the room, a massive window overlooked the forest. The view would be spectacular in the daylight, but right now the sky and forest were dark with only a hint of moon gleaming on the leaves.

I faltered to a stop in the bathroom.

Arrow paused and smiled. "Nervous?"

"Yes." I licked my lips. I couldn't explain it. I'd never in my many times of using men experienced nerves over sex. This was only sex. I shoved my anxiety away and lifted my dress up and over my head in one swift action.

"Honey," he rumbled.

His voice echoed through the bathroom and bounced off the walls, raced up my spine, and traveled to my ears. Time to get this heat back to sex. To stop ignoring the incessant throb between my legs just to hear the deep rumble of Arrow's voice. His sexy words and his demands to get to know me. Disregard the reaction deep inside my chest that wanted to tell him more about me. To have him know me as someone other than a sexual partner.

No more 'getting to know' Arrow. No more sharing, apart from our bodies. This was what I was here for. Nothing else. No. Nothing else.

"Touch me, Arrow."

"I'll touch you until you're begging me to stop."

I shivered at his promise.

"Hop into the shower and I'll join you after I brush my teeth. Don't want my meat breath over you, do you?"

"No, I don't." My shudder of revulsion may have been exaggerated.

"I'm not giving up meat." Determination filled his words.

"I wouldn't expect you to. I'm here for a short time."

His golden eyes narrowed, and his jaw set in a firm line of clenched teeth. I walked to the shower before I examined his expression and my reaction to saying I wasn't here for long. I opened the large glass screen door to a shower large enough for Arrow and me. The stone walls and gray square tiles looked almost like a rock's surface. Stepping inside, I turned on the taps until the water ran warm and pelted my sensitized body. I couldn't wait for his touch on my bare flesh. I longed to see Arrow naked and to rub his skin against mine.

My heat roared back with a vengeance in a long, low swirl. I wished it to be me wanting Arrow without the heat. *Would the appeal be the same? Would he still desire me without the overpowering pheromones?*

The shower door slid open and Arrow stepped in with a rush of cool air. I twisted to the magnificent specimen of a man. Burnished skin covered an abundance of muscles, two glorious pectoral muscles scattered with dark hair, six perfectly defined abdominal muscles and a trail of hair leading downwards from his belly button. I dragged my gaze to his intense eyes. His thickly corded neck worked on a swallow. The veins on his large biceps thudded as fast as my pulse. No wonder he'd carried me with ease. I slid my gaze downward, wanting to see all of him. His cock was hard, more veins ran along the sides of his thickness. His broad head flared and swelled further under my gaze. Lower still, his balls peppered with dark hair drew tight, full, and ready to fill me again. Underneath, his thighs bulged with more muscles and another spattering of hair. I couldn't wait to feel the sensation of his hair on my sensitive skin.

I ran my fingers up his arm, over his chest, and downward, following the direction my gaze traveled. His skin was warm beneath my caress, enticing and tantalizing. I stepped forward and pressed my body against his. Our combined groans echoed in the shower.

"Saoirse. Your touch is insane."

I grabbed his firm ass cheeks and squeezed. "I craved to touch you the moment you stepped into the bar."

"You didn't want Sledge?"

"No, I desired you."

"Good." He tugged my hair, giving him access to my mouth.

He touched his minty lips to mine and demanded entrance. I opened to Arrow in a way I'd never opened to anyone. His tongue sought and rasped against the length of mine, twisting and twirling as his tongue had earlier against my clit. I grew lightheaded with his plundering kiss. His teeth nipped at my bottom lip. I gasped in pleasure and he sucked my lip into his mouth.

I dug my nails into his shoulders, trying to anchor myself and not float away on the sensation. Float to new heights of sexual pleasure. I'd performed many sexual acts before Arrow, but it was different with him.

He released my lip and lowered his head to my nipple, drawing the taut tip into his mouth.

"Aye," I cried.

He sucked and rasped my nipple with his tongue until I tugged on his hair, then he brushed the elongated tip with his teeth before switching to my other nipple. I tilted my head back. Water washed over us both in our little world of desire. My nipples were sensitive to the spray of the shower above us. My power burst free yet again, but the fall of the shower's water covered my rain.

I coiled tight on the blinding ecstasy. Arrow's fingers and mouth roved my damp body. Everywhere but where I desired them most, neck, breasts, hips, stomach, thighs, even my ankles. I ached with desire. Hollow without him inside me. My body trembled, ready and poised.

He turned me around and kissed the back of my neck. A jolt of sheer pleasure almost made me pass out. His lips skated down my back, over my buttocks, and along my thighs. A long rasp of his tongue on his way back up along the inside of my thigh. He spread my cheeks with his hands and ran his tongue over my slick folds, over my puckered entrance, and up my back.

"Arrow," I moaned.

He brushed my hair off my neck and nibbled on my earlobe.

"Yes?"

"I want you now."

"You do?"

"Aye." I shoved my hips back until my ass touched his hardness.

He grasped my hands and pinned them to the wall. Then he kicked my legs apart and slid into me with a knee-wobbling thrust of his enormous cock.

"Oh, my..."

He set a rhythm somewhere in the middle of not fast enough and not slow enough. Mind-numbing pleasure keeping me high and never letting me go, never letting me fall over the other side of the peak and into the free-fall of orgasm.

"Faster," I cried.

"No," he said with a growl. Fiery breath brushing my neck and ear.

"Slower." I said, begging.

"No."

My desire spiraled higher at his demanding voice.

"I can't take it." I sobbed.

"You can." He squeezed my hands against the wall. "You will."

"Aye," I said, giving myself over to Arrow.

"I said you'd be screaming for me to stop and not stop. You're not there yet."

"I am." I screamed.

The water cascading over us turned cool. *Were we in the shower so long we depleted the hot water? Or is my power out of control?* I didn't care.

"Stop," I said, no, screamed.

Arrow chuckled and stopped. I quivered and jerked under his body. I felt him buried deep. A part of me. I wanted him. All of him.

"Don't stop," I said, now commanding.

He hissed, long and low, and started his torturous pace again. In and out over my sensitive flesh. He drove me into the wall. My nipples hit the cold tiles in ecstasy. My aching clit touched the cool tiles, too. One brush and I'd explode, but he kept my hands pinned above our heads while working me with his cock.

His thrusts grew harder, more demanding, marking me more on the inside than any man ever in all my years. I dropped my forehead to the tiles. The pleasure grew to a peak of insanity.

"Please." Now I was begging.

Arrow rasped his tongue along my neck, then bit my tender flesh. Everything exploded at once. A long pulsing intensity from deep inside, rippling in waves over and over, swarming me, surrounding me, marking me.

I screamed. Arrow howled and joined me in the release. The rumbling sound through his body made my orgasm more intense, the deep pulsing squeezed harder and tighter still. Blood roared in my ears. I couldn't suck in oxygen. I let the pleasure take me on its ride. Beautiful and perfect.

As the potent waves petered to soft ripples, I drew my power back in.

Arrow slid free, sending a shudder along my spine. He released my hands and turned off the taps, then ran a caressing hand over my back while I gasped for air. My heart beat a rapid tempo inside my chest, but Arrow's constant caress brought it back to normal. He placed a gentle kiss on my shoulder. I swung my arm back and caressed his head, keeping his lips against my skin. He took the hint and nibbled the tender flesh, drawing a lazy, contented sigh from my re-oxygenated lungs.

"You truly like doggy?"

"I told you it's my favorite." He chuckled.

It was now my preferred position, too. Although it might only be because of Arrow.

"You're so honest." I yawned.

His hand halted in his caress.

"Dia, you are an intense lover. I almost passed out."

"Let's get you into bed, then."

He scooped me up into his arms.

"Arrow, I can walk," I said.

"I enjoy carrying you." He strode from the bathroom.

"Your hero complex coming through?" I settled into the warmth of his arms.

"Something like that," he mumbled.

"Shouldn't we dry off first?"

"Nah, it's hot enough we'll dry off in no time, and I like you wet."

"Arrow." I slapped his chest lightly.

He responded with a quick kiss to my lips and tumbled us onto the bed. He rolled me over and spooned me from behind, enveloping me in his heat. True to his word, the damp moisture from the shower dried in no time. My eyelids fluttered closed. He was so warm and comforting at my back. His firm arms circled my waist and dragged me even tighter to his body. The embrace made me feel even sleepier than after my last orgasm.

"Arrow?" I said into the darkness.

"Hmm," came his rumbling reply, sounding every bit as sleepy as I did.

"I've never done this before." My voice came out quiet, as though the revelation told him everything he needed to know about me.

"What? Gone home with a guy you picked up in a bar?" he teased.

"No. I've done that," I scoffed.

"What then?" His warm breath brushed over my nape as he moved closer still.

"I've never slept with them in bed like this," I admitted.

"Ah." He hugged me tighter.

I settled into his arms.

"That makes me happy."

He nuzzled my neck. A thousand sparks of sensations flared across my body. A warm glow filled my heart that I'd made him happy while my body basked in the rightness of being held in his arms. I wished there could be more to this moment. More between us.

"It does?"

"I'm pleased I'm your first for something."

"I'm glad it's you who's the first." And I was, for Arrow had shown me more care and consideration than any man ever had.

His arms stiffened around my waist, the hairs prickling my stomach.

"What's wrong? Do you want me to leave?"

"No, I don't want you to leave. I want you to stay."

It was my turn to stiffen. I couldn't stay. Fae weren't welcome in the mortal realm. The Trappers taught us humans feared and despised us for our power. People didn't want us on Earth. They'd attempted to burn us all alive, to steal our powers, to kill us. Arrow might be the same if he realized the truth, I was a Fae princess.

He brushed a hand through my hair and plucked a flower from my crown. "What's with the flowers?"

"I like flowers."

He placed the flower on the pillow in front of me. "They smell identical to you."

"Fancy that."

"Yes, fancy that," he drawled. "One day you'll tell me your secrets."

I sighed. One day I might if I stayed longer, but I wouldn't be on Earth to yearn for more. More of him, and to have Arrow for me. A Fae with a human? Impossible after our history.

I shut my eyes, letting his heat cocoon me with the ever-present lust, comfort, and a desire for more. My breathing deepened. He stroked his fingers through my hair in a constant caress, lulling me toward sleep.

"Your hair is silky."

He'd woven a spell around me, wrapped in his safety. I released a sigh of contentment and drifted away to the darkness of sleep.

"Sweet dreams, my mate," he said.

CHAPTER TEN
ARROW

I WOKE TO MY mate snuggled in my arms, her head on my chest. Her hair spread across me like a living silk sheet. Heaven. Pure in its simplicity and the rightness of mating. My dick twitched, but we needed more than sex between us.

"The best way to wake up." I kissed the side of her head.

She sighed and snuggled deeper into my embrace. I never wanted to let her go. I wouldn't. She might think she'd leave in a few days, but I needed to convince her otherwise.

"There's somewhere special I'd like to take you today."

"Can't we stay in bed?" She wriggled in my arms.

"We can... or I can show you something extraordinary."

I eased my hold on her, and she rolled to my side. I kept an arm around her shoulders and rubbed the bite mark on the back of her neck. My claiming mark. The mating mark which sealed us together forever.

"Extraordinary? I'm intrigued."

"I hoped you'd say that. It's my favorite place in the world. I think you'll love the spot, too."

"You think you know me?"

She sat up, and my arm dropped from her body. The loss of my mate's touch was instantaneous. She shifted her leg a fraction, so she touched me again. Seemed the mating bond worked on her, too.

"Not yet." I sat up and brushed her hair back from her face. "I want to though."

"Why? Why can't this be about sex?"

"Honey," I said, "sex is great, and sex with you is phenomenal, but there's more to life than sex."

The indigo ring around her eyes shone. She glanced away and gazed out the window overlooking the expanse of the forest I called home. The forest I couldn't wait to show her and the hidden gems inside. There was a magical wonder to Crystal Creek, and I wanted to share the joy with my mate.

"I'll pack a picnic basket, and we can take a rug to my special place."

She didn't answer me. I resisted the sigh welling in my chest.

I brushed a hand down her bare back. "Please, Saoirse? Let me share this with you."

I couldn't stop touching her. I caressed her back over and over until she relaxed and said, "Okay."

A minor victory and I'd take the chance to show Saoirse how we could be so much more together. I rose from the bed before I did what she wanted and stayed in bed with her all day.

"I have spare clothes you can wear."

She stood on the other side of the bed and stuck her hands on her hips. "You said you didn't have a girlfriend."

The jealousy pouring off her made my heart pound with excitement. I might not have to battle to keep her as much as I thought.

"I don't. They're my mom's clothes. She, um... keeps clothes here... in case there's a wildfire, and she loses her house."

I wanted to wipe my brow with my stupid explanation, but the excuse was the best I could come up with on the spur of the moment. I should have contemplated it before I offered her the clothes every shifter kept at their house in case another pack member needed them after a shift.

"Do you have many fires here?" She relaxed, dropping her hands from her hips.

"Some years we do. Depends on the weather. This year has been exceptionally dry and hot. We've already experienced multiple wildfires."

"And you fight these fires?"

"I do, with my team, and other firefighters."

She tilted her head. "Do you like fire?"

"No, can't say that I do." I stepped over to my closet.

"Then why fight them?"

I yanked on boxer shorts. "If I don't, who will?"

She rounded the bed. "Maybe you're not meant to."

"What do you mean?" I stepped into a pair of jeans and tugged up the zipper.

"I'm not sure." She shook her head, flinging a flower from her hair. It fell to the floor.

I bent and picked up the delicate bloom and placed it on the top of the drawers.

"Do you intend to keep all the flowers that fall from my hair?"

"Every single one."

She smiled shyly. The first unsure smile I'd seen on her face.

I slid a white t-shirt over my head.

Saoirse's smile changed to her sultry one. "I can't decide if I prefer you with clothes or without."

Laugher rumbled from deep in my chest. My mate was something else.

"I prefer you without, in case you were wondering." I met her sultry smile with one of my own. "But I can't have you wandering around my favorite place naked. Come with me to the spare room and you can choose what to wear."

"Good to hear you prefer me naked."

She followed me into the spare bedroom and opened the closet.

"Your mom won't mind me wearing her clothes?"

I didn't tell her they weren't my mom's clothes. That would require more explaining. Like how I'm a wolf shifter, how I'd marked her without her permission. A part of me still felt like an asshole for that, but I'd been powerless to stop my wolf from claiming her. Powerless against the allure of my fated mate. I wanted to build a connection between us first before I dropped that on her. Plus, my mom should be happy I'd found my mate, but with Saoirse being a Fae, well, I wasn't sure how she'd react. Some older townspeople held a grudge against the Fae for disappearing after wiping out the Trappers and turning humans against all supernatural beings. I'd never met a Fae in my life. The stories of their existence were like a fairy tale these days. I couldn't wait to introduce everyone to my mate. What happened to the Fae was long before I was born.

But others remembered.

How and why was Saoirse here? What secrets was she hiding? Apart from the fact she hadn't told me she was a Fae. *But why would she?* I needed to earn her trust. I had to get her to talk to me.

"Arrow?"

I snapped out of my deliberation with a start. "They're new clothes. I can always buy more. Pick whatever you want, I'll go pack a picnic."

I strode from the room before my mate saw into my churning emotions. I didn't doubt she was the one for me, but others might have a problem with a Fae in town.

My mom might be one of them.

Leaving Saoirse to dress, I rummaged through the refrigerator and put together a delicious feast for our picnic, conscious of the fact she was vegetarian. A meat-eating wolf shifter with a vegetable-eating Fae. *What were the odds of fate putting us together as mates?*

I had nothing to compare our relationship with. Most of the mated wolves I was aware of mated with other wolves. Outside of Crystal Creek, immortal creatures mixed matings on the occasion, but it was more normal to mate with a creature of the same species.

I shoved the food into a backpack along with a soft blanket and towels and hooked the straps over my shoulders. Saoirse padded into the kitchen on her bare feet, dressed in a pair of tight denim shorts and tank top hugging every luscious curve. My mouth watered to lick every delectable inch of her pale skin. I skimmed her form multiple times before forcing myself to concentrate on something other than pleasuring my mate.

"The shoes didn't fit?" I asked.

"I don't like shoes."

"It's a bit of a trek through the forest. Are you sure you don't want shoes?"

"I'll be fine."

"All right, let's go." I placed my hand in Saoirse's and led her through the house, out into the welcoming forest.

She wrapped her fingers with mine in an easy way she'd accustomed me to in a small amount of time.

The sun was well and truly high in the sky, its summer intensity blaring on our heads until we disappeared under the coolness of the shade of the large gum trees. A magpie warbled in the distance, and another responded. My wolf settled into the peace of the forest and urged me to change and run through the undergrowth in the way we normally journeyed to our destination. He was excited to show his mate our special place.

"It smells so exquisite out here," she said.

"That'd be the eucalyptus leaves you're crushing under your feet. They give off a soothing scent. It's why I love it here. Do you have eucalyptus where you're from?"

She plucked a long, slender feather-shaped leaf from a tree and lifted it to her nose.

"No eucalyptus trees where I live."

"And where do you live?" I couldn't help asking.

"Somewhere different." She tucked the leaf into the pocket of the denim shorts she'd chosen to wear. "We have lush forests with tall gray barked trees and leaves of gold, as high as a mountain."

"What type of trees?"

"Populus tremuloides. I believe you call them Pando or the Trembling Giant."

"Do you know a lot about trees?" I asked, curious she knew the botanical name for the trees in her home.

"No, but my sister Briana does. She has an affinity for nature."

"And you?"

"Me what?" She frowned.

"What do you have an affinity for?"

She met my searching gaze. "I guess you'd say water. I love lakes and rivers. Freshwater waterways. Saltwater is, well, too salty."

I laughed. "That it is. There's no saltwater this far inland in Australia. We have a lake and a creek that runs into it. But you already know that, don't you?"

I didn't want to spoil my surprise by telling her where we were going. Especially now I was certain she loved the water.

"Aye." She ducked her head. "I saw your lake when I arrived in town last night. It was quite beautiful with the mountain range on the other side."

"It is. I often swim in the lake. Do you like to swim?"

"I do. Back home we have a giant blue lake surrounded by the greenest fields of lush green grass, but the lake is dwindling in size, swimming is nigh on impossible now."

"That doesn't sound good for your hometown."

I held a branch aside, and she ducked through the small gap. The track through the forest to my special location wasn't well-traveled, and I typically ventured this way in my wolf form.

"It's not good." She pursed her lips. "It's been nice to get away from home and the problems there."

I followed through the gap and let the branch go. "I'm glad you came here."

She turned and smiled. "Me too. This trip has been the best I've ever experienced."

I smiled and tugged her hand down to half crawl through the small gap between the bushy trees.

"Last bit, then we're there."

I crawled through first, not very chivalrous, but I wanted to see her face when she saw the waterfall for the first time. The rush of the water traveled to my ears like there was a spell around the waterfall to keep its location a secret that even the sound couldn't be heard unless you were inside the circle of eucalyptus trees surrounding it. I wouldn't be surprised if there was magic concealing it in the same way magic concealed our town.

I scooted across the dusty soil and rose in a rapid spin to capture the expression on my mate's face.

She didn't disappoint me.

Her pale blue eyes grew large, with the indigo ring shining brightly. They glistened with the reflection of the water gushing over the rock face in a steady stream of white-blue. I knew the scene like the back of my hand. How the water would fall into a turquoise pool with frothy bubbles underneath. How the sunlight streamed across the face of the rocks in a golden haze conveying a mystical quality to the place. All around, the trees cocooned us, held us safe and sacred to the sight of the waterfall.

Saoirse gasped. "What is this place?"

"Sona's Waterfall."

"Sona, as in meaning happiness?"

"I'm happy here." I wrapped my arm around her shoulders and gazed at the sight I never grew tired of seeing.

"So am I." She sighed. "I need to touch the water."

"Go on then." I let her go and waved at the water.

"Are you coming in?" She unbuttoned her shorts and dropped them to the ground.

My gaze dropped to the sight of her bare legs and lifted to the creamy abundance of skin she revealed when she yanked her tank top off over her head. I scrubbed a hand over my jaw. She hadn't worn underwear, but she hadn't when I met her.

She lured me with her sultry smile.

"Absolutely," I said, grabbing the hem of my t-shirt.

CHAPTER ELEVEN
SAOIRSE

T HE AZURE WATER SURGED toward me like a magnet pulling on metal. Ripples ran rings around my body and tickled my chest. I swirled my hands under the surface where Arrow couldn't see and coaxed the water to run over my limbs in a soothing caress.

"Dia, this water is exquisite."

"It is," Arrow said wading into where I bobbed. "I come here as often as possible."

"I'd live here." My power surged like a living current beneath my skin, as the waterfall charged me from the inside out.

"You can't live in water." Arrow chuckled and reached for me.

"Watch me." I laughed, flicking water his way, before swimming across the pool to pause underneath the flowing force of the waterfall. The water reminded me so much of our spring back home when the water flowed with this much gentle force except there was no Fae life force running through this water.

Arrow swam to me in strong powerful strokes of his muscular arms. He reached me, a wicked grin stretching his lips, and wrapped his hands around my waist. My body flared to life with the slight contact. We bobbed under the waterfall enjoying the smoothness of the water running over our heads and down our backs. I let my power free, like it urged me to do, and added a misting rain to the running water of the waterfall. Arrow peered up at the misting rain, then slammed his lips to mine.

We kissed for an eternity underneath the falling water. We kissed like we couldn't stop kissing. Like a power inside us both forced us to stay locked with our lips.

This man was incredible.

Never in my secret trips to Earth had I experienced anyone like Arrow. I dug my fingers into his shoulders. I wished we could be more. If only he were a Fae, then I could take Arrow back to the Summer Court with me. I'd mark him as my mate and Father would stop his request I mate with Tadgh.

If only.

But Arrow wasn't a Fae. He was human. If I marked a human with the power of a Fae mating mark it might end in his death at worst, or at best, a lifetime coma, and what would be the point then? I couldn't have Arrow for more than here and now. Mating with him was impossible.

But we had the here and now. I wrapped my limbs around his waist and urged him closer still. Closer than

I'd been with any human or Fae. My power flew out in a wild ecstasy and drew on the waterfall, making the water run swifter and more intense over our sensitized bodies. We moaned into each other's mouths but kept our lips joined.

I couldn't let Arrow go, but I'd have to leave him.

One more day of this heaven on Earth with Arrow and then I'd return to the Summer Court. Back under my father's demands and being Saoirse the Fae princess instead of Saoirse the woman Arrow wanted.

I'd never been more myself than when I was with Arrow. I wished I could tell him I was a Fae princess with unimaginable powers over water. If I did, I could stay with him, have him accept my words as the truth, have him make me feel this special for the rest of his life.

He broke the kiss.

I hissed.

"Be with me," he said.

"I couldn't be anymore with you than I am right now."

"Here." Arrow cupped the side of my head with his palm. "You're not."

How did he read my mind? Like he comprehended my scattered thoughts lay elsewhere instead of with him and how I felt in his arms. And, Dia, I felt so much in his arms.

"Arrow."

The fall of cold water didn't faze him even though his skin was cool beneath my touch. It was as though his focus was on me. On my comfort. His concern was about me and what made me happy.

"Saoirse." He smiled with his full lips.

"Arrow." I returned his smile.

"Saoirse." He grinned with a flash of his teeth.

I sighed. His teeth. I wanted his bite again. I longed for the rightness and connection his bite instilled in me.

"That's better." He brushed my damp hair with his fingers. "You with me now?"

More than ever, I was.

"Yes."

"What do you want?" His skin pebbled into goose bumps.

I licked the cold water from my damp lips. There was much I wanted, but the one thing I wanted more than anything I'd ever wanted in my life was Arrow.

"I want you," I said.

He brushed my wet hair back again. A shiver of need wracked my body. Every heated touch was Arrow. He lowered his lips to the curve of my neck and nuzzled the sensitive skin. Every nip of his teeth was Arrow. His lips trailed up to the edge of my lips. I sought his mouth in a ravenous kiss. Every kiss of his lips was Arrow. His tongue danced with mine. Every stroke of his tongue was Arrow. I gripped his firm back and let him sweep me up into the delights of him. A small part of me realized I let him do more than have sex with me. I let him claim me with his hands, his mouth, and more. I'd longed for a moment like this for many years. But with Arrow I didn't have to wonder. My heart warmed as each beat pulsed a rightness through my body. Maybe a human was meant to claim me.

Perhaps it would convince my father humans and Fae could coexist once again. That he could unlock the veil separating our two worlds and let Fae choose if they'd like to visit Earth.

Although the wrath of the Fae king wasn't something I wanted to experience.

Arrow tugged my hair, stopping my mind from wandering again. He bared my throat to his mouth and bit my neck in the way I'd longed for all day.

I cried out with the zing of pain from his sharp teeth heightening the pleasure pulsing over my body. Arrow growled. The sexiest sound I'd ever heard rumbling against the sensitive skin on my neck.

I gasped for breath.

"Look at me," he rumbled.

I met his glowing golden gaze. A depth of lust and more swirled in the gold and black of his eyes. Something tangible, but unidentified. Whatever was in his heated gaze sent my heart racing and my body free.

He licked my neck with a rasp of his tongue then brought his golden gaze to mine. I ran a hand over the rough stubble on his jaw and cupped his cheek. Long moments passed while we studied the other's face like we both needed to memorize the other's expression.

It was me who first broke the connection, and I flicked my gaze to the calm ripples of the waterfall in the pool.

"I wanted to swim," I scolded with no compunction behind the words.

"I told you I preferred you naked. Expect me to ravish you whenever you walk around naked in front of me."

He released me from his hold and waved his hand at the pool. All I wanted was for his arms to hold me again.

"I'll, ah, have to remember." I shoved off from the wall.

"Don't worry, honey, I'll remind you every day."

I dove under the water. *Every day. Dia, did he think I'd stay here?* I couldn't stay. It wasn't possible even if I wanted to stay on Earth. Which, maybe I did. Aye, stay with Arrow, enjoy his attention, his incredible pleasuring of my body, and the rightness whenever we connected as one.

Not to forget his bite. His teeth did things to my body I'd never experienced before Arrow, but it wasn't feasible with who I was, what I was, and who my family was. Not to forget the problems we faced as Fae. No, the odds were insurmountable.

The water coaxed my body into calmness and soothed my churning emotions. I broke the surface of the pool with reluctance I'd have to face Arrow and our short time together. I should have left today as soon as I woke. A dark shadow passed through the leaves of the lower branches in the trees.

"What was that animal?" I spluttered.

"What?" Arrow asked standing on the shore already dressed in his pants.

I rubbed my eyes and the droplets of water from my eyelashes. "I saw a wolf."

"A wolf, huh?" Arrow slipped on his t-shirt.

"I must be seeing things. Wolves aren't an Australian animal, are they?" I swam to the edge of the pool and peered into the undergrowth of the forest.

"No, they're not." Arrow paced to the line of the trees, a scowl on his face.

"Arrow," I called out. "Be careful."

"Are you worried about me, honey?"

He paced back smiling and offered me his hand. I placed my hand in his but shrugged off my concern because concern meant more than sex and I couldn't let that happen. I wouldn't show him I longed for more with him than sex. That was all we had. All I could give in the short time I spent on Earth.

I ignored the warmth of his palm in mine and the tingle of awareness traveling up my arm and across my neck to his bite mark.

"I'm hungry. How about our picnic now?"

CHAPTER TWELVE
ARROW

O F ALL THE DUMBEST things Sledge had done, coming to the waterfall in his wolf form while I was here with Saoirse had to be the number one. *What possessed him to venture this close?* I scowled into the forest. I sensed his gaze watching from a distance. *Didn't he trust the Fae even though she was my mate?*

How long had he watched us?

If he'd seen my mate naked, then I'd have to rip his balls from his body and shove them down his throat. My wolf raged in possessiveness that another wolf was so near his mate. He wanted free to chase off the other male. A loud warning growl escaped my curled lips.

Saoirse jerked back and scrambled from the water without my help.

Shit.

"Sorry." I patted a hand to my stomach. "I'm starving. Let's eat."

I tossed her a teal green towel from the backpack I'd carried to the waterfall. She caught it midair and rubbed herself dry then dressed in a hurry. When I thought I was on my way to winning her over, she retreated again. She dangled the towel from her fingers and peered into the forest. She wouldn't catch sight of Sledge again. He'd be careful now.

I stepped away from Saoirse and spread the picnic blanket over the soft soil by the banks of the waterfall. With a stretch of my denim-clad legs, I settled on the plaid rug and opened the backpack.

Saoirse walked to the edge of the clearing and peered even harder into the forest like she would see Sledge. *As a Fae, would she see further than a human? Further than a wolf shifter? How powerful were the Fae?* I'd learned all there was to know about us 'others' from the elders in town but seeing a Fae in the flesh was a whole other experience.

"Saoirse, honey, come eat with me, please?"

She flicked her long white-blonde hair over her shoulder and made her way over to me. With one last glance back at the woods, she settled on the rug in front of me.

"I think an animal is out there."

"There are plenty of animals in the forest. It was probably a kangaroo you saw."

"Perhaps." She frowned. "I could have sworn it was a wolf."

Maybe now was a good time to broach the subject I was a wolf shifter?

"I like wolves," I said. "Do you?"

"I have an empathetic connection with them."

"In what way?"

"Humans fear them and hunt them. Oh." She slapped a hand over her mouth.

I slid my hand up her arm and tugged her hand away from her mouth. "Did someone hurt you?"

She blinked her long lashes quickly. "A long time ago."

"I'm sorry."

"It wasn't your fault, Arrow."

"I know." I rubbed the back of her hand with my thumb. "It upsets me to think of you in pain, and it makes me want to do bad things to anyone who hurts you."

"You're so sweet." She tangled her fingers with mine.

I chuckled. "I want to hurt people on your behalf and you think it's sweet."

"It's sweet where I come from and it would please my family you'd defend me against harm."

"And you, would it please you?"

"Aye, Arrow. You please me."

"I enjoy pleasing you." I shuffled closer to my mate. "I especially like watching your face when I please you."

Saoirse wriggled on the blanket, her shorts riding up her thighs even higher and giving me a glimpse of the creamy silkiness of the limbs she'd wrapped around me.

She dropped her gaze to the growing bulge in my pants.

Saoirse licked her lips. "What's in the bag?"

I whipped out a banana instead of my semi-hard cock.

"I'm happy to see you," I said waggling my eyebrows.

She laughed so lightly, the sound hit me square in the chest. She retrieved the banana from my outstretched hand. Her shoulders relaxed and dropped to their natural position instead of tense and up around her ears after watching the forest for a shadow of a wolf. *Was it the idea of a wolf that bothered her or the notion of being watched?*

I withdrew a buttery croissant from the bag. "For you, my lady, a croissant with tomato and basil, and for me a croissant with bacon, brie, and honey."

"My, you are a domesticated man, aren't you?" She raised her eyebrows.

I laughed. "I'm the furthest from domesticated you could ever get, but I like good food."

"Who taught you how to cook?"

"My mom did. She wanted a daughter, so when she ended up with a third boy, she was determined to inflict me with all the knowledge she wanted to pass onto a girl."

Saoirse bit into the croissant and chewed. "What else did she pass onto you?"

"Oh, boy. Do I have to say?"

She nodded, her pale blue eyes lighting and the indigo ring adding to the mischief swirling in the depths. She shifted closer and ran a hand over my leg.

I bit into my croissant, ignoring the thrill of her touch on my leg, and chewed. Saoirse waited for me to stop chewing.

I sighed. "Fine, but don't tell anyone else."

"It can't be terrible, you're an amazing man." She took a bite of the croissant.

"Mom taught me how to sew. I can make clothes, darn socks, you name it, I can sew it."

Saoirse laughed so hard she slammed a hand over her mouth to keep the food from flying out.

"That's not all, besides cooking, and sewing, she made me watch chick flicks with her."

"Chick flicks?" She frowned.

"Movies about women, most of them about romance. Then she'd talk about them with me afterward."

She giggled. "Did she talk to you about girls?"

"Good grief, yes, when I was a teenager, she handed me her favorite romance novel and told me this was how I should treat all women. She didn't prepare me for the graphic sex scenes in that book."

Saoirse finished her croissant and shifted into my side wrapping her arm around my waist. "I think they were the best thing for you."

I tackled her to the ground. She squealed in laughter. I gazed down into her amused face. Shit, I'd fallen fast for my mate. She was beautiful and funny, and sassy. Sexier than any woman I'd been with.

"Bet you won't find that move in a romance novel." I kissed the tip of her nose. "Tell me something embarrassing that happened to you when you were that age."

Her eyes sparkled. "My mother used to sing at masquerade balls. Her and father would dress up in gorgeous clothes and delicate face masks. I wanted to go with them so much that I threw a tantrum when I was around a similar age."

"A tantrum at that age?"

"What can I say, I wanted to go." She grinned. "Little did I know the ball was for, oh, um, matchmaking."

Arrow chuckled.

"My grandfather was there and told me what the ball was for, which then lead to Father having a talk with me about sex." She covered her eyes with her hands. "It was so embarrasing listening to my father tell me those things."

I drew her hands away from her face, my lips twitching the entire time as I attempted to hold in my laughter.

"Go ahead and laugh," she encouraged me. "But it gets worse."

"Go on," I encouraged.

She filled my heart with hope with the ease she was telling me this story. That she was at last opening up to me.

"A few years later I made Lorcan try to sneak into one of those balls with me."

"What happened?"

Her cheeks flushed a delicate pink.

"Sir Axis, the man running the ball found us skulking at the entrance and took us inside right up to our parents and told on us. He thought it beyond amusing we were there, even more so when he saw the look of horror on Father's face since we were both still too young for that sort of party."

"What did your father say?"

"It wasn't what he said, it was what he did."

"Which was?" I asked, eager to catch more than a glimpse into her life.

"He made Lorcan and I work on a farm in my mother's hometown."

"How was that worse?" I frowned.

"Because the farms he made us work on was a horse breeding stud. Those animals are huge." Her cheeks turned bright red.

I threw my head back and let out a roar of laughter. Saoirse laughed with me. Her happiness was all that mattered to me now. I cupped her face between my palms.

"Your poor impressionable mind. Do men measure up after that experience? Or were you left disappointed?"

She grinned. "I'll never tell. Now where did the banana go?"

"Happy to see me?" I drew her up into a sitting position otherwise I'd lay all day with her in my arms.

"I am." She lifted the banana in her delicate hand.

I picked up a flower from the rug which had fallen from her hair with my tackle and inhaled the fragrance that was all Saoirse. She wrapped her lips around the banana. I regretted my decision on the choice of fruit with her plush lips wrapping around the phallic shape, the glint of lust shining in her eyes, and the teasing flick of her pink tongue.

After agonizing minutes, she finished the fruit. I flung the skin away and urged her onto my lap.

She didn't complain. She didn't stop me. Saoirse wanted me to touch her with the same urgency and all-consuming need that overran my senses, scrambled my brain and made anything but thinking of pleasing her impossible.

I'd never get enough of Saoirse, but Sledge was still out there watching us.

What I cared about was my mate.

Shit, I needed to stop lying to Saoirse about what I was, and what we meant to each other, but I was worried how she'd take the news. There was more to Saoirse than I understood. She guarded herself well, too well. Someone had hurt her in her past and she'd retreated bit by bit, I lured her to reveal more and trust me. My stomach knotted at the worry that the truth would break the fragile bond we'd formed and she would think we weren't compatible as a wolf shifter and a Fae. My wolf whimpered she might not want to be my mate.

But fate made us mates.

If I accepted it, wouldn't she?

"Tease," I said.

She brushed her hair from her shoulders and smiled with her innate sultriness.

"You like it."

"I do." Gathering her in my arms, I nuzzled her neck. "I like you."

A rustle of leaves came from behind us. Saoirse scooted out of my lap and clenched her hands at her sides. The waterfall appeared to run faster in a louder splash against the pool underneath.

I rose and flipped my middle finger up behind my back. Damn Sledge for interrupting again.

"Let's head home, it's getting late."

We gathered the blanket and damp towels and stuffed them into the backpack. I slung the straps over my shoulders and threaded my fingers with Saoirse. Together we made our way through the forest as the lowering sun cast shadows skittering through the branches. A small gray kangaroo bounded across the track in front of us. Saoirse started. I hauled her close and rubbed her back.

"Easy, a little kangaroo won't hurt you."

She huffed out a shaky laugh. "Sorry."

"You're not scared out here with me, are you?"

"No," she scoffed squaring her shoulders. "I, ah, I'm a tad unsettled."

"I'll keep you safe."

She chuckled and rolled her eyes. "I'm more than capable of keeping myself safe."

"Do you know self-defense moves?"

"You could say that." She tugged my hand. "My father taught me how to defend myself against attackers."

"He sounds like a good dad."

She walked a dozen steps before replying. "He is in his way."

I adjusted the strap on the backpack. "And your mother? What's she like?"

She smiled. "Mother is like a chocolate-covered candy. Sweet on the outside with a hard inside."

I laughed. "Do you like candy?"

"Aye. It's a treat I enjoy when traveling."

"How about we laze in front of the television and I'll show you my mom's favorite chick flick and feed you candy?"

We pushed through the last trees in front of my house and walked up to the front door.

"I won't say no to candy."

I opened the door for my mate.

She stepped up to me and molded her body against mine. "Candy, chick flick, then I need you naked again."

"Honey, sounds like the perfect night."

I kissed her sweet lips, drowning in the feel of my mate, the taste of my mate, the essence of her connected to me with my bite.

I trailed my lips to her ear and said, "Chick flick first."

"Tease," she husked and strode into the lounge room swaying her hips in enticement.

I scrubbed a hand over my rough jaw, I should shave but Saoirse enjoyed the bristles rubbing against her skin and I enjoyed marking her in any way I could with my body. By the time the night was over, I'd mark her in as many ways as possible.

CHAPTER THIRTEEN

SAOIRSE

I WOKE DISORIENTATED. THE room was dark. The bed beside me was cool. Arrow's body heat was absent. Two nights in his bed and I'd never been more at peace. I should have left yesterday but I couldn't do it. I drew in a lungful of his dark scent and calmed my racing heart. Images flittered through my mind of my dreams. Sharp teeth, golden eyes, rippling skin, hard muscles, and then softness. I rubbed my forehead in confusion.

What was happening to me?

I rolled over in the gigantic bed. Fresh scents drifted in from the open door of cooking. Delicious aromas making my stomach rumble in anticipation. Arrow cooking again. *How hungry was he?*

A gleam of light shone through the doorway and showed me the way in the darkness. I slipped from the bed, snagging his shirt hanging on the doorknob, and shrugged into it, not bothering with buttons. I desired Arrow again. All our times together were...

I shook my head. *What were they?*

It was more than sex while I'd been in heat. We'd formed a connection.

I staggered from the room with the realization I'd developed feelings for Arrow, feelings other than lust which concerned me. Feelings for a human. I paused at the end of the hallway and leaned against the doorjamb.

Arrow filled the kitchen with his presence in the dominating, controlled way he'd filled me. Become a part of me. *What would I do? How would I leave him?* I didn't have a choice. If I stayed in the mortal realm, he'd discover my secrets, my true identity and it would horrify him. I'd outlive him too. My brothers and sisters would come looking for me sooner or later. And Father, I didn't want to think of what he'd do.

"Hey." Arrow paused catching sight of me in the doorway. "What are you doing skulking over there?"

"I'm enjoying the view." I smiled.

The view was spectacular—Arrow in boxer shorts. An abundance of his burnished skin was on display. His muscles rippled while he shuffled about the kitchen. But what made me smile the most was seeing him with a jar of peanut butter in one hand and a spoon in the other hand.

"Hope I didn't wake you. I was hungry."

"You're insatiable."

I shoved off the doorjamb and walked into the room.

He chuckled. "Honey, you've no idea."

He passed his tongue over his teeth and dropped his gaze to the open front of his shirt on my body. I shivered in longing to have his intoxicating bite again.

"Come here." He placed the jar and spoon on the counter and crooked his finger my way.

I padded across the tiled floor and stood toe to toe with him. He lifted a hand to my hair and wrapped the strands in a fist and tugged until my head fell back. His lips landed on the base of my neck and he scraped his teeth along my tingling skin.

"Arrow," I moaned.

He slid his other hand inside the open shirt to my waist and yanked me flush against him. His heat coated me, and his lips met mine for a branding kiss of tongue and teeth making me whimper in need.

He broke the kiss and smirked. Then he lifted me on the counter.

"Lay back, honey, I want to eat you for breakfast."

I did as he said, eager for Arrow to do whatever he chose to my body. No man ever sated my needs like Arrow. My heat was over, the need to have a man satisfy me absent. This need tugging at my insides was for Arrow, but my time on Earth was at an end. I'd already stayed longer than I should have.

He brushed the sides of his shirt open to reveal my eager nipples.

"You're spectacular."

I expected him to latch onto their eagerness, but he lifted my legs and placed them on his shoulders. Then lowered his face to my damp core.

"So wet." His warm breath skated over my slick folds. "Is this for me?"

"Aye," I panted. No lie. This insane need was for Arrow.

His gaze met mine, and he flashed a toothy smile before rasping his tongue over my sensitive flesh. I kept my gaze on him, knowing he wanted me to watch. I desired to witness the way his gaze grew heavy with pleasure while he licked me over and over. Threading both hands into his hair, I held on, while he tumbled me over the edge into a thigh shaking orgasm in record time.

He dropped a kiss on my stomach. "I love the way you taste."

Love? He released my legs. They hung over the counter's edge in boneless limpness. I dropped my head back on the counter and stared at the ceiling. *Love?*

Get a grip Saoirse, he didn't say he loved you.

I sat up with a start and slid from the counter.

"Are you...?"

"Am I what?" He lifted an eyebrow.

"Do you want to...?" *What the shite was wrong with me?* It was sex. That's all. *Wasn't it?*

"Do I want to what?"

Why was I so nervous?

I lifted my shoulders and met his gaze. "Do you want me to reciprocate?"

He smirked, his pointed teeth sitting on the edge of his lips. "That was for you, honey. You don't need to do anything you don't want to."

I swallowed hard. Never had anyone, Fae or human, said that to me. Arrow was turning me inside out and making this heat into more than sex and lust. More than using a man to slake my requirements. He'd surpassed my necessities and met ones I wasn't aware existed. If only he could be my mate.

I licked my lips. I should say something, anything. He gazed at me with expectation. Of what I wasn't sure. I'd never been unsure of anything with men before Arrow.

When the silence stretched beyond a reasonable time for me to respond, he softened his smile and stepped away from me. The loss was instant. His heat, essence, dominance, and gentle caring. He picked up two plates from next to the cooker.

"Come outside with me for breakfast."

"Outside?"

"I watch the sunrise with breakfast every morning, and we slept through it yesterday. It's calming to watch the sun's rays' stream through the trees."

I nodded and followed him through the house to the front porch. Arrow tipped his head at the swing seat and I slid onto the downy cushions in the gloom of the early morning. He sat next to me, his thigh brushed mine, and his leg hair tickled. He draped a blanket across my legs before placing a plate on my lap.

"You cooked for me again?"

"Blueberry pancakes. Hope that's okay."

"More than okay." I kissed his cheek. "Blueberries are my favorite fruit."

He turned his head and tugged my bottom lip into his mouth with his teeth.

"I wanted to have a nibble before I eat meat and need to brush my teeth again."

I laughed. "You'd clean them for me?"

"I'd do anything for you, Saoirse. I realize we met a short time ago, and the sex is amazing, but it's more."

"More?" I gulped.

"I can't explain it. I want to, but I'm not sure if you'd believe me."

"Why wouldn't I believe you?" I frowned.

He shook his head. "You might not want to believe me either."

"Arrow?" My voice quavered.

"Hey, it's okay." He brushed my hair. "It's nothing bad. You can trust me. I won't hurt you. Let's eat breakfast and watch the sunrise and then I'll tell you. Deal?"

His golden eyes pleaded with me, and I nodded.

"Deal."

He placed a kiss on my forehead and dug into his plate. I tore a piece of pancake from the pile and put the fluffy goodness in my mouth. Delicious flavors burst free from the plump blueberries over my tongue. The first rays of sunshine lit the sky. Golden streaks, reminding me of Arrow, stretched through the branches and leaves. Birds woke chirping and tweeting, singing the new day into being.

The entire time I was conscious of Arrow. Of his heat, and allure. His presence and essence filled me with a sense of calmness and completeness. I ignored the panic at what he wanted to say. *I can trust him, can't I?* I'd trusted him with my body. My head and my heart were another matter, yet somehow, he'd wedged inside. He'd found a way inside me and I didn't want to let him go. I wanted more of him.

"How old were you when your father and brothers died?"

"Thirteen. Old enough to grasp the extent of the fire, but too young to help. Mom dragged me to the lake with the other town members not fighting the fire. We have fires almost every year."

"Every year!"

"The Australian forest is so dry in summer. Eucalyptus trees are highly flammable too. They're a part of our country, fires. They can be helpful to remove undergrowth and encourage fresh growth if executed in controlled conditions, but when they happen by themselves..."

I squeezed his hand. "Tell me about your family."

"My father was a larger-than-life man. He was big, bigger than Sledge, but underneath his size was a soft heart. He always made time for his kids to kick the football and run through the forest together at night."

"You run through the forest at night?"

"Oh." He ran a hand through his hair. "Yeah, it's a family tradition."

Family tradition. I sighed. The Fae Royals seeped our family tradition in making sure the royal line continued to lead our people.

"What about your brothers? How old were they?"

"My brothers were much older, in their late twenties. They'd been fighting fires alongside Dad since they were sixteen. They were experienced firefighters, I guess that's why their deaths stung so much, because they shouldn't have—"

"It wasn't their fault."

"I know." He took my empty plate and placed it on the ground with his, then wrapped an arm around my shoulders.

I leaned into him and laid my head on his chest. This was so much more than sex, and this would be my last time with Arrow. I wanted to learn as much as possible about him before I stepped through the veil and returned to the Summer Court.

"It stung to be left behind." His deep voice rumbled against my ear.

So honest. I slid my hand across his stomach caressing the ripple of his muscles with each ragged breath he inhaled. Guilt settled in my heart. I'd leave him behind too, but I couldn't take a human to the Summer Court. He wouldn't pass through the veil, and if by some miracle he did, then the Fae King was liable to kill him on sight.

"I was younger than them, but they never let me feel like I was less. They showed me a thing or two on the sly without my parents' knowledge."

"Like what?"

"Like how to kiss a girl."

I laughed. "At thirteen years old?"

"Yeah, at thirteen." He chuckled.

"How old were you when you had your first kiss?"

"Twelve, and it was dreadful. The entire town heard about how awful the kiss was and that's why my brothers helped me, so I wouldn't tarnish the family name again."

"Tarnish the family name?" I raised both eyebrows.

"It was a reflection on their masculinity if their younger brother couldn't kiss."

"Oh, you poor baby." I laughed.

He kissed me then, and I didn't care he'd eaten meat. He showed me without a doubt he could kiss the sense out of me, and his brother's teachings worked, there was no tarnishing his family name. With the way he kissed, his family name would be legendary.

He broke the kiss and scanned the forest, stomach muscles growing tense under my palm. Leaves rustled, and I peeled my gaze away from Arrow's clenched jaw to his narrowed eyes.

His friend Sledge stepped through the trees.

CHAPTER FOURTEEN
ARROW

"**S**ORRY TO INTERRUPT," SLEDGE said. "But you're needed at the firehouse."

I tugged the blanket higher on Saoirse. "But we have a few days off."

"We did, but something has come up that needs the captain's attention."

I peered into the forest behind him but I couldn't see any other pack members out there lurking in the undergrowth.

"I'm busy."

Saoirse placed her hand over mine. "It's okay, Arrow. You have a job to do."

I glanced at Saoirse then at Sledge. Everything that felt right since my mate appeared in my life without warning felt wrong. I rubbed my jaw.

"Why didn't you call?"

"I did. You didn't answer," Sledge said.

"Shit, I must have left my phone inside."

Sledge eyed Saoirse.

"You remember Saoirse." I stood and dragged her up with me.

"I do," he said. "It's good to see you again."

"Hello." Saoirse dipped her head. "I'll head inside and get dressed."

"I'll come with you." With a death glare at Sledge, I ushered her inside the house. "Back in a few minutes."

"No worries." Sledge kicked a rock across the driveway.

I let the door slam behind us.

"Is everything all right?" Saoirse asked.

"Yeah, sure, I'm bummed about leaving you. I shouldn't be long though. If there was a fire, my beeper would have paged me."

We walked into my bedroom. The tangled mess of sheets where we'd slept the last two nights together, a reminder fate meant us to be together. I dressed in my uniform. Saoirse sat on the bed and examined me.

"You're very sexy in your uniform."

I laughed. "You're very sexy in my shirt."

"Yeah?" She bit her lip.

Where did the sultry, seductive woman go? Right at this second, she was so unsure. *Was it because I told her we needed to talk?*

"Yeah. You're sexy in clothes, sexy out of clothes. I said I wanted to talk to you, and I haven't had the chance with Sledge rocking up, but when I get back, I promise we'll talk."

"Okay," she said.

I frowned. "Are you okay?"

"I am."

Her quiet words didn't ease my concern. I stepped toward her.

"Arrow, dude, let's go," Sledge called out.

I growled. "I'm coming."

Saoirse stood from the bed and kissed my cheek.

"Thanks, Arrow."

"Thanks? What are you thanking me for?"

She shrugged. "Do you mind if I take a shower while you're gone?"

"Go right ahead, honey. Make yourself at home."

"Thanks," she said again and padded to the bathroom.

"I'll see you later."

She paused at the door and threw me a smile over her shoulder. "Bye, Arrow."

"For fuck's sake, Arrow," Sledge called.

I stormed through the house. Sledge leaned against the front door, his massive arms crossed over his chest.

"About time," he said.

"I wasn't long."

He straightened and opened the door.

I stormed outside. "Who said you could come inside, anyway?"

"Since when is your best friend not welcome to wait inside your house?"

"Shit, sorry, man. I..." I scrubbed a hand over my jaw.

"Yeah, I get it. I've seen enough recently mated shifters to understand what you're going through."

I yanked open the door to my truck. "I've seen them too, but I never imagined mating would be this intense."

"Yeah, dude, I've never seen you so close to losing it before."

We climbed into the Ranger, and I drove down the long dirt road. I flexed my hands on the steering wheel. Every second away from Saoirse was like a gaping wound.

"You, um, seem to be getting along well," Sledge said.

"Enjoy your peep show yesterday?" I raised an eyebrow.

"You were swimming when I arrived."

"Good. So why were you spying on us?"

"My dad sent me." He rubbed his thick thighs. "He doesn't trust the Fae."

"And you?"

"I don't know any to form an opinion."

"Good answer." I flicked my gaze to Sledge for a second.

"She seems nice so far."

"She is." I swung around another bend. "If I didn't know better, I'd say she was human."

"But she's not." Sledge pointed out.

"No," I agreed.

"And she's not a wolf shifter."

"No."

"So, the pack might have issues." Sledge tapped his fingers on his thighs.

"I figured that would be the case. Is that why I'm requested at the firehouse?"

"Yes. Good old Dad sent me to fetch you when you didn't answer your phone. He figured I'd be the least likely for you to rip to pieces."

"He's right. I might have contemplated ripping your balls off yesterday for spying on us, but I probably wouldn't have."

"Gee, thanks," he drawled.

"You wait, Sledge, when your mate shows up, you'll see exactly how intense this reaction is."

He snorted. "For one, I don't want a mate, for two, where will I find a mate around here? The shifter pool is so small here, it'd be like mating with a cousin."

I grimaced. "I know the sentiment. You never know, your mate might wander into town like mine."

"Heaven forbid another Fae wanders in here. Dad would think they're declaring war."

"Who said your mate would be a Fae?" I stopped my truck in front of the firehouse.

"No one." Sledge jumped out and stormed up the four steps into the building.

With an annoying little niggle in the back of my mind, I followed Sledge into the one-hundred-and-thirty-year-old brown brick firehouse. The garage alongside the building housed the fire trucks. Inside the building I knew as well as my home, the entire shifter town stood in the dining hall.

Shit, this would not go well.

"Do you know if the Fae means us harm?" the Alpha, Ray Braidwood, asked stepping forward.

A murmur rippled through the crowd.

"She's just a woman," I said.

"No Fae is just a woman," the Alpha commanded the attention of the room. "What did you find out from her?"

I scrubbed a hand across the stubble on my face. "She's vegetarian."

"Are they all?"

I shrugged. "I didn't ask."

"But it would be safe to assume they all are?"

I shrugged again, tired of this interrogation already.

"There has to be more."

"She has brothers and sisters."

The Alpha scowled. "What about her power? What is it? How does she use it?"

"For fuck's sake," I muttered. "I didn't take the time to ask her those questions. I mated with her, and well..."

"You mated?" He stepped back. "You're no use to us then."

"What do you mean?"

"Your loyalties are divided now." His jaw clenched with an annoying tick.

"My loyalties have always been to my family." I scanned the crowd looking for my mom, but she wasn't there. "Where's Mom?"

"Marianne is on a pack assignment." He waved both hands like it was the least of his worries. "I understand what the wolf shifter mating bond is like. If there was a decision between your pack or your mate, you'd choose your mate."

"Why are you painting her as a bad guy? She's done nothing wrong."

"Yet."

I threw my hands up in the air. "Whatever happened to innocent until proven guilty?"

A few murmurs of agreement rippled through the crowd. I squared my shoulders.

"Look, I might not understand much about Fae, but I've sensed no malice from my mate. She never wielded her powers or did anything to make me think she would hurt us."

Sledge stepped up to my side. "I sensed no threat from her either."

"Are we bigoted? Aren't we all immortal creatures with powers of our own? Why should we discriminate against a Fae because we haven't seen one in years?" I puffed out a breath. "Look, how about some of you meet her? See for yourselves she's no threat to our pack."

"Fine, Arrow," the Alpha said. "A few of us will follow you home and meet your Fae mate."

"Now?"

"Got a problem with that?" He folded his thick arms over his chest. "Or do you want to warn the Fae we're coming?"

"No, it's not that. I haven't told her I'm a wolf shifter yet."

He spluttered. "How did she accept your mating mark if she didn't realize what you were?"

"She just did."

Another murmur rippled through the crowd. It was unheard of for a wolf shifter to mark their mate without explicit consent and discussion beforehand. Except

Saoirse gave her consent the first time we'd met, the first time I'd asked her if I could bite her.

"How can she be here to hurt us if she doesn't realize what we are?" I asked.

"She could've been fooling you. She could've seduced you to get to the pack. Saoirse might want to kill us all as they did to the Trappers."

I laughed hollowly. "Do you hear yourself? What they did to the Trappers was warranted."

Now, more than ever, I wished Sledge would take over the role of Alpha. His father was obnoxious sometimes.

"I have the pack's best interest in mind."

"Whatever." I waved my hand at the door. "Let me take you to meet this killer Fae you're so afraid of."

I stomped out of the firehouse. Never in my life had I felt unwelcome in this building, but the Alpha's fear throbbed through the room like a living creature. I'd show him. I'd show them all Saoirse wasn't to be feared. She was one of us now. She was my mate.

Sledge jumped into my pickup truck with me. I churned up the gravel road as I roared my engine and spun the wheels.

"Let's not crash on the way there," Sledge said.

I eased my foot off the accelerator. "This is fucking ridiculous. Saoirse wouldn't hurt the pack."

Sledge tapped the window. "Hard to tell if you haven't talked to her about being a wolf shifter."

"Are you on your dad's side?"

"Hell, no," he scoffed.

"You know we can scent lies."

"You know I'm not lying then," he said.

"Thanks for having my back."

"Anytime." We fist-bumped.

I slammed on the brakes and slid to a stop in front of my cabin. My chest swelled with the intense desire to hold Saoirse in my arms again and protect her from this stupid idea of the Alpha's.

"Let me talk to Saoirse first, before you all barge into our house."

"I'll keep Dad out as long as I can."

I nodded my thanks and swung open the front door. Saoirse's scent lingered like the first rain of the season, but while her lingering scent was here, I knew with absolute certainty she wasn't in the house.

"She's not here." I swung the door shut. Lifted my nose to the air and followed her scent into the forest.

Sledge trailed me scenting the air at the same time.

"She's heading to the lake," Sledge said.

Water. She loved the water. She smelled like water. I suspected her power was over water. *Was she, as the Alpha feared, about to use her power to hurt the pack?* I didn't believe that for a second.

As we followed her scent, the blue lake shimmered into view. Imprinted in the sandy soil of the bank were Saoirse's bare footprints. We followed them to the water's edge where they disappeared.

"Is she swimming?" Sledge asked.

I scanned the horizon of the flat lake. No ripple of movement broke the serene water. The dread filling my chest when I'd first opened the door settled like a hard lump of certainty and turned my heart to stone.

"No, she's gone."

"Gone where?" Sledge lifted his hand to shield his eyes from the sun and stared across the lake.

"Gone back to wherever she appeared from, probably." I shoved my hands into my pockets.

"And where's that?"

"She said the other side of the lake, but I doubt it." I swallowed. "The Fae are more well-hidden than us."

"Shit, man, I'm sorry. I'll go tell Dad. Then we'll check out the other side of the lake just in case."

I dipped my head but couldn't speak through the lump in my throat. Saoirse told me she was here for a few days. Two days of the best sex I'd ever enjoyed. Two days of getting to know my mate.

Two days was all it'd taken for me to fall in love with her.

Sledge left and returned. My gaze never left the lake. I willed Saoirse's form to swim through the glistening blue water, splash me in the face, laugh, and tease me with her sensual lips and body.

A hard slap on my back jerked me from my dreams.

"Dad's pissed," Sledge said. "He spurted some bullshit about you warning her he was on his way and that's why she left."

"Fuck." I scrubbed a hand through my hair.

"I informed him, not too gently, that I was with you the entire time and you didn't so much as twitch a finger to alert the Fae we were on our way."

"Thanks," I mumbled not giving a flying fuck what the Alpha thought when my mate was gone.

"Do you want to do this in wolf form?"

"It doesn't matter either way. I ingrained her scent in my senses, and her scent ends here at the water's edge."

Sledge stripped his clothes and tossed them on a fallen log.

"Let's run. It'll help your wolf let off his frustration."

I grunted and stripped my clothes.

Sledge's body shimmered in a black haze of rippling fur and contorting limbs until he landed on the sandy soil in his black wolf form. The wolf inside me gave an excited yip and lunged to the surface in a flash of golden fur. I padded to the side of the larger black wolf. In this form, Sledge was superior to me as the direct descendant of the Alpha, but as with our firefighting, we always had the other's back. I nudged his side with my head in gratitude. Sledge bound across the shore of the lake and into the forest.

I darted after him. With each soft pad of my paws, my wolf settled into being, resolved into finding his mate. A mate he knew as I did, we wouldn't find. The enigma of the Fae presented itself to us as a problem we never considered.

Eucalyptus leaves crunched under my paws. Branches brushed against my soft fur. *What would it be like to show Saoirse my wolf form? Would she have left if I'd shown her? Told her we were fated to each other?*

Sledge whined. I loped up to his side. We'd traveled to the other side of the lake, I'd been so lost in thoughts of Saoirse I hadn't noticed the distance we'd covered. This side of the lake was more wild and untamed than the side we lived on. A kookaburra laughed from a tree above us.

I dropped my nose to the print in the silt beside the lake and snuffled at the delicate, almost not there mark.

Sledge contorted into his human form and squatted at the imprint. I changed too, so I wasn't staring at his junk.

"It's not Saoirse."

"Well, duh," Sledge said. He traced a finger over the top of the print. "It's not a wolf either. See the pads of the toes, they're closer than a wolf, and there are no claw marks."

I studied the one smudged impression of a pad with four toe prints. "It's almost like a big cat's print."

"Yep." Sledge stood and scanned the tree line around this side of the lake.

I spun and searched the low-lying bushes. A prickle of awareness skittered up the back of my neck.

"A big cat in Australia?" I asked.

Sledge laughed. "The same as wolves in Australia."

He had a point. "A shifter? That's even more unlikely."

Sledge folded his arms. "As unlikely as you mating to a Fae?"

"Shit." I rubbed my bare foot across the print and erased the evidence. "Whoever, whatever it is, it's got nothing to do with Saoirse. She's not on this side of the lake. I know it. My wolf knows it. She's gone."

"Gone where?"

"Fucked if I know."

I shifted into my wolf, let out an almighty howl of pain, and raced into the shadows of the forest. I wouldn't outrun the pain of losing my mate, but maybe if I exhausted myself enough, the pain in my limbs would outweigh the pain in my heart for a few blissful minutes.

CHAPTER FIFTEEN
SAOIRSE

A S SOON AS ARROW'S vehicle drove away, I stripped off his shirt and donned my dress. The silky Fae material was alien to my body after a mere few days on Earth. Being here felt as right as being in the Summer Court, and with Arrow, it felt righter still.

I shoved the feelings aside and ran through the forest before I did the unthinkable and stayed on Earth. *How was I entertaining the idea?* I'd never wanted to stay before. Before Arrow, there'd never been this aching need to stay.

The eucalyptus leaves crunched under my feet, brushed against my arms, and sent up a waft of the peaceful aroma. The same scent I'd always associate with Arrow and our first time in the forest. When I next returned to Earth, I'd come here. I sighed. If, I returned to Earth. With Father's request hanging over my head, I might not return for a long time, and then Arrow would have aged, maybe even died.

I stumbled with the last reflection.

Dia, what happened to me?

My emotions concerning Arrow were unprecedented.

A rustle of the leaves in the forest crunched to my right. I paused and scanned the dense foliage. When no other sound emanated, I ran the rest of the way to the lake. It was better if I left now without a proper goodbye. I'd said goodbye knowing I wouldn't see Arrow again. The guilt in my aching heart that he believed he'd come home to me almost made me turn around. Almost made me stay in the bedroom to start with.

I burst through the trees and onto the sandy shore of the lake. With a wave of my hands, the air shimmered, and I eased apart the veil separating our two worlds. Enchanting in a swirling, shimmering haze of blues and indigos, much like the water underneath the veil. If I possessed the time, I'd stand on the shore and watch the veil revealing itself to this world with the magical wonder of our Fae power, but I didn't have time.

I slipped through the veil as a wrench on my heart like a piece of me stayed behind with Arrow. My neck burned. I rubbed a hand to the places Arrow bit me in the thralls of passion.

The veil shimmered with its power. I stepped into the atrium of the palace inside the Summer Court.

"About time," Lorcan said.

"Lorcan?" I wiped the backs of my hands over my cheeks, surprised to find them wet.

"Are you crying?"

I staggered into his arms and sobbed.

"Shite, Saoirse, what happened? Did humans hurt you? Do I need to go through the veil and rip heads from bodies?"

I hiccupped and sobbed.

Lorcan patted my back. After my crying eased, he shifted me back and ran an assessing gaze over me.

"What are these marks on your neck from?" He touched one with his fingertip.

A jolt of power zinged from the mark into my neck. Lorcan must have sensed the zing too because he frowned.

"Saoirse talk to me. You tell me everything."

I scrubbed my face dry. "I met a man. He was a little bitey in bed."

"And?" He waved his hand.

A small fire sparked to life in his palm.

"He didn't hurt me. He was good to me. Too good."

"Oh."

He closed his fingers and extinguished the flames.

"I think I have feelings for him."

"Shite, Saoirse."

"I know, I know." I paced the atrium. "How could I with a human? After everything they did to us."

"There's nothing you can do about him, anyway. You're home."

I stopped pacing. "Except Earth felt like home. He felt like home."

Fire danced along the length of Lorcan's fingertips. He studied the flickering red and orange flames.

"Do you think the human is your mate?"

"No, it's not possible. Is it?"

Lorcan shrugged.

I called my power to my hand coating my fingers and palm in a glove of water and placed my hand on his, dousing the flames into a sizzling hiss.

"It's not possible," I repeated.

Lorcan nodded. "Father thinks you've been with Tadhg."

My eyebrows rose. "How did you deceive him?"

"I bribed Briana to entertain Tadhg in your place."

"Do I want to know what you bribed Briana with?"

"No, you don't. Let me say, you're not the only princess with secrets you want kept."

"Oh, Lorcan." I wrapped my arm through his. "How was your groupie?"

"Same as the others." He sighed in exaggeration. "Clinger all the way. They all recognize I'm not actually looking for a mate. Shite, no one in the Summer Court has mated for years."

"I know." I rubbed a hand to my neck.

"You need to cover those when you see Father."

"Won't he think they were from Tadhg?"

Lorcan peered closer at the mark. "They're not the same shape as Fae teeth."

"And you comprehend this how?"

Lorcan smiled with a toothy grin. "How else?"

"Dia, you're such a cad."

He snapped his teeth together. "Yet, you love me."

"I do, Lorcan, you're the best brother."

"Better than Rian?"

"Way better than Rian and his overbearing big brother shite. Although, he's mellowed a fraction the last few years."

Lorcan laughed. "He's overbearing with all of us. I've thought the same thing, I wonder if he's getting laid with regular occurrence these days?"

I laughed. "Anyone would think he's the king with the way he acts."

"Father has groomed him for the throne."

We made our way into the palace interior through the grand marble halls toward my bedroom. Mother rounded the corner in a flourish of her royal purple dress and white-gold flower crown. Lorcan and I ground to a halt. Her gaze dipped to my neck, then widened.

"Lorcan leave us."

"Yes, Mother." He bowed and scurried away.

"Saoirse get in your room now before your father sees you."

She grabbed my arm and marched me to my room with a speed I'd never witnessed from her before. She hauled me inside and locked the door behind her.

"I don't know how you'll hide this from him." She strode to the window and drew the drapes across.

"Hide what?"

"Don't play innocent with me. The mark on your neck tells me all I need to know. You forget when my family were alive, they were happy to form relationships with others beside Fae."

"It was my heat."

Her back shot ramrod straight. She marched to the door and paused with her hand on the doorknob.

She spun around. "How could you go there? After everything that happened to us? Do you not remember that night?"

"Of course I do," I hissed. "Seeing you burned so badly I thought you'd die is forever etched in my mind."

"Then why go to Earth?"

"You know why."

We stared at each other.

"Mother." I sighed. "We need to find a cure for the spring."

She placed a trembling hand to the base of her head, her fingers unerringly moving to the darker red strands beneath the silver-blonde that had stained her hair after her near-death experience.

Her bottom lip trembled. "You can't go there again."

"Earth has changed since you were last there."

"I'll never trust humans again. What they did..." Her eyes glistened with tears. "I don't know how we'll tell your father about this. What will he say? After everything he's done to protect us."

"Father doesn't need to know."

"I won't keep secrets from him. I'll give you time to tell him before I do, but don't take too long."

She shook her head and slipped through the door in a silent way that reminded me of my younger sister Ciara.

For the first time in centuries, my palace bedroom didn't feel like home. I sunk onto my bed and stared at the closed door. Mother's words worried me. I walked over to the mirror hanging over the crystal mantlepiece and studied the marks on my neck. *What was so special about them?* They appeared like any other lover's bite mark.

Except they were Arrow's.

My heart was back in his house. Back in the place that now felt like home. The many years of living in the Summer Court were like a prison, but now I appreciated what and who was out there, it felt more like torture.

If this was how I suffered a few hours away from Arrow, how would I survive hundreds of years?

The turquoise lake of the Summer Court glittered under the stream of yellow sunlight piercing the fluffy white clouds. So much was similar yet different between the two worlds. In Crystal Creek the trees were gray limbed and green-leaved. The trees here were golden with shimmering silver bark. The water in the lakes was different blues. In the sky, the blue was sharper, more intense. The clouds were always white. The seasons were always mild. Nothing changed in the Summer Court.

Except now I'd changed. I saw the Summer Court through fresh eyes. With a different need pulsing in my body and an ache in my heart.

I dipped my toes in the water. How I wished the lake was deep enough to swim in still. I'd love to experience the difference in the water between the Summer Court and Earth. Then I'd know for sure this place was home.

I called a stream of water into my hand with my power and viewed the crystal blue droplets dancing in the sunlight.

"I knew I'd find you here," Rian said.

"Did Lorcan send you?" I kept the water dancing.

"He's worried about you. You've been hiding from everyone for weeks."

"I've been hiding from Father after Mother acted bizarrely about... never mind."

"About the mark on your neck?"

The water dropped with a splash into the shallow lake. Droplets flicked over my pink dress and Rian's beige pants leaving splotches of dark wetness.

"How do you know about them?" I touched a hand to the soft pink scarf wrapped around my neck. Since Mother's reaction, I'd kept the mark that wouldn't disappear even though it had healed covered at all times.

"May I?" He pointed at my scarf.

I nodded and unwound the scarf until nothing covered my neck. Of all the ways I'd expected my oldest brother and next in line to the Fae throne to react, his smile of happiness wasn't one of them.

"You're happy?" I asked, gaping at my brother.

"I am." He unbuttoned the top three buttons of his golden-yellow tunic and tugged the edges down to reveal a bite mark on his neck.

"You have the same bite mark too?" I stepped closer and peered at the similar yet different mark on my brother's neck.

Rian examined my bite mark with a swipe of his cool finger. "Similar, but yours are different. I've seen your type many moons ago before the Trappers and before we ended up locked in here."

"Of course, you have. They're a human bite mark. We don't associate with humans now."

"Human?" He raised both eyebrows.

I scowled and wrapped the scarf back around my neck. "Arrow was human."

"Are you sure? I'd swear they're—"

"They're what?"

"Ah, never mind. It's not my place to say such things." He re-buttoned his tunic and spun away.

"Rian." I called a massive drop of water from the lake and hovered it over his head.

Rian glanced up and using his power, he shifted the rich soil into an umbrella over his head. He smirked.

"I'll win," I said.

"Try me," he goaded.

I dropped the water on his head, dousing the dirt and turning it to mud. He laughed but remained dry. I flicked my hand at the water and flung a wave in his direction. He shifted the soil into another barrier thwarting my effort but turning his dirt into mud. The mud landed on the bank of the river.

"I'm not telling you." He ducked my next throw of water and flicked mud at my feet as though he'd stomped in the puddle.

"Why not?" I sidestepped the mud.

"It's not up to me. You need to talk to the man who put the mark on your neck."

"I can't," I whined and swiped another wave of water at Rian. "He's on Earth."

"So?" He blocked the water again and flicked more mud at my feet.

"Stop it."

"Stop what?"

We both flicked water and mud at the same time resulting in them colliding and landing in a puddle at our feet, splashing our legs. A smile tugged at the corners of my lips. Play fighting with our powers was childish, but it was so much fun to still enjoy this time with my brother.

"I said you wouldn't win."

"You didn't win either," I huffed.

"Ah, but I did. I won the greatest treasure of all. I wish I could tell you more, but it's not the time." He gazed across the lake then turned back to me. "Don't you see, Saoirse? The mark has more meaning than you think. You've forgotten the old days. Forgotten what it means. The power behind marking a lover."

I touched a hand to my neck. "Power?"

He nodded. "Power is everything. We hold power, but there is a greater power out there. One that is more powerful than being a Fae royal."

I scanned around the quiet shore. "Don't let Father hear you speak that way."

"Father." Rian scowled. "He's forgotten too."

"What have we forgotten?"

"Everything." Rian shifted his hands. The veil between Earth and the Summer Court shimmered in a bronze haze.

I gasped. "How are you breaching the veil here and not at the spring?"

"Our power is greater than we believe. We can do this anywhere, anytime. We can go to Earth anytime we choose. He can't stop us."

"We've always been so secretive of our trips to Earth while looking for the source of the spring. Why didn't you say anything sooner?"

"I couldn't. Still can't. I'd like to share them with you, but if Father found out." He shook his head. "It's too great a risk."

"What's a risk? You're not making any sense, Rian."

"One day you'll understand. Maybe sooner than I imagined now you're marked too. Now you've found—" He placed a hand in the veil. "I'm visiting Earth. Would you like to come?"

I peered to the left, then the right. Not one Fae traveled to the lake anymore, the place was too dry, too barren, too much of a reminder of what we were losing every day in the Summer Court.

"I do, but I want to go somewhere special."

"I'll take you to your man."

"How did you know?"

"I know a lot, princess." He bopped me on my nose.

I swiped at his hand, but he was too quick to swat away.

"Stop. I'm not a kid."

"I'm the oldest. You're all little kids to me." He laughed and waved his hand at the veil. "After you."

I stepped up to the shimmering bronze and gold veil. Excitement bubbled in my stomach and made my heart pound in anticipation I'd see Arrow again in mere minutes. Everything felt like an eternity in the Summer Court. *How much time had passed on Earth for Arrow?* Time passed unusually in the Summer Court.

Rian stepped up beside me. "Think of who you want to see and you'll end up coming out of the veil right next to him."

"What about you?"

"I have someone I want to see."

He passed through the other side of the veil and disappeared. Cryptic Rian. When I saw him next, I'd be sure to get answers out of him like who did he want to see. Right now, my focus was on Arrow. Seeing Arrow. Talking to Arrow. Touching Arrow. Kissing Arrow.

Everything was Arrow.

And then I stood before him.

CHAPTER SIXTEEN

SAOIRSE

I STEPPED THROUGH THE shimmering veil in front of Arrow's familiar log cabin. The dawn broke in his favorite time of the day casting rays of golden sunlight streaming through the trees like caressing warm fingers. The perfect time to see him again. Arrow lifted his golden eyes and raked my appearance from head to foot.

My body heated from his intense stare. My body flushed with a surge of welcoming, and yet I was no longer in heat. This man was my...? What?

"Arrow," I said.

"You left."

I dipped my head. "I did."

"Why?"

I tugged on the silky material of the scarf and unwound it from my hot neck. In Arrow's presence, the bite mark he'd left on my neck warmed and tugged like it wanted me to step closer to him.

"I, ah, I."

"I thought we had something special," Arrow said. "Something more."

A lump formed in my chest. We'd enjoyed something special. More than passionate sex. Arrow made me feel things, want things, and I'd run home like always.

"I want to talk."

"I wanted to talk the day you left." He jumped off the swing seat. "You disappeared for a week. Why did you leave? Why didn't you say goodbye at least?"

"Arrow." I raced up the stairs and grabbed his arm. "I'm sorry I left the way I did."

He stared at my hand. I let go of him. I didn't have a right to touch him anymore after leaving him the way I did, with no goodbye, no explanation. Nothing.

"My life is complicated," I said. "I'm not who you think I am."

He shifted to face me. "Who do I think you are?"

I shrugged. "A woman who picks up men in bars."

Arrow growled a dark rumble from deep in his chest.

I stepped back.

He snapped out a hand and snagged the end of my scarf. "Don't run from me again."

"Arrow," I muttered.

He tugged me closer until his breath coasted over my cheeks and fluttered against my eyelashes. "You can't leave me again." His words came out like a pain-filled plea.

"I don't want to."

"Then don't." He slid the scarf from my neck. His golden gaze roamed with blazing hunger over his bite mark. "You're mine."

"I think I am, but I need to explain to you about myself. I'm not sure you'll understand."

"I need to tell you more about myself too." He dropped my scarf on the porch. The silky material fluttered to the timber like delicate butterfly wings. "Tell me after I kiss you. I need to have your lips on mine. Tell me you want to kiss me too."

I dragged my gaze to his sinful lips. The lips which kissed me like no man ever did. The lips which pleasured my body in so many unique ways.

I nodded my head.

Arrow leaned closer until his dark, masculine scent filled my lungs.

"Say it."

"I want you to kiss me," I said without hesitation,

I wanted his kiss more than I'd ever wanted anything in my life.

His lips landed on mine. A scorching kiss. A declaration in every thrust of his tongue. A claiming in every tug of his teeth. The kiss devoured me. Ignited me. Inflamed the mark on my neck. Flooded me with desire.

I fumbled for the zipper of his pants.

Arrow groaned.

In the background of my heightened senses, a car door slammed. Then another, and another. Arrow stopped kissing me to glare at the newcomers.

A tall, slender, woman with long dark hair hanging to her waist, tanned skin, and golden flecks in her intense eyes glared at me. Alongside her two pretty, brunette young women radiated the same hostility.

"Mom, when did you get back?" Arrow's eyebrows rose.

A growl rumbled from the woman, his mom. The hairs on my arms stood on end. The warning was distinctly aimed at me. I removed my arm from Arrow's waist and shifted out of his embrace. Arrow clenched his hands at his sides.

"Don't."

"A Fae princess," she growled. Her skin rippled and pulsed with power.

I jerked. *How did she recognize what I was?*

"I said don't." Arrow rumbled.

Her nostrils flared the same way Arrow's did, the resemblance uncanny, but then she changed. Her body contorted, a shimmer of dark gray with flecks of gold, her clothes ripped in a loud tearing noise, stilling the forest creatures. She dropped to her hands and knees, fur rippled along her naked body, her face elongated, and became a wolf.

The gray wolf glared at me with death in its eyes.

Instinct took hold. I ran.

My bare feet hit the dirt flinging up clouds of dust, but I'd never outrun a wolf. The gray wolf slammed into me from behind, knocking me to the ground and smacking my head against the solid earth. Her paws and claws dug into my back. My power unfurled, ready, and willing to protect me, but her weight disappeared from my body. I gasped, the knock taking the oxygen from my lungs too.

A loud ringing exploded in my ears, the escalating growls beside me added to the confusion. I rolled to the side. Two wolves appeared from nowhere. A gold-coated beast of a wolf standing between me and the smaller gray wolf. The female wolf's gums twitched back in a snarl. White fangs snapped in my direction.

The golden wolf stood unmoving. My protection against the angry gray wolf. The golden wolf was familiar. My protector. Every rumbling growl sounded like Arrow. Arrow was the wolf. Arrow was my lover, my...

Sleepy words drifted back to me.

My mate.

I lifted a hand to the back of my neck. The first bite mark. The mark that didn't vanish even though it was healed. If it wasn't for my heat, I would have known this was more than a bite. *What did he do to me?* I stared unseeing. A Fae princess mated to a wolf shifter. *What did I do?*

The growling halted, but I didn't care. I drowned in the enormity of my actions while they regained their human forms.

"You mated?" His mother gasped.

"Yes," Arrow half rumbled half spoke, the wolf still clear in his voice.

"Oh, sweetheart, I'm so sorry," she expressed her regret.

"It's not me you need to apologize to."

"You're right."

Unable to deal with the moment, I dragged my knees up to my chest. I couldn't stay here on Earth. I couldn't be Arrow's mate. No matter if I desired to.

"Saoirse." Arrow scooped me into his strong comforting arms. "Are you hurt?"

Hurt? Am I? My body, no. My emotions, aye. I'd let Arrow into places I'd never let another male, and he was a wolf shifter. *How didn't I sense he was an immortal?* My damn heat, that's why.

"Honey, answer me."

His commanding tone never failed with me.

"No," I said.

He drew me to my feet using his incredible strength and ran caressing hands over my shoulders and down my back, checking for himself his mom didn't injure me. The woman's pleading eyes met mine over his shoulder as she stood a short distance away. I didn't know what to make of her. Of this situation.

"I'm sorry she acted like that." He kissed my forehead. "Ready to meet my mom?"

I shook my head.

He chuckled. "You two got off on the wrong foot, but it's my fault. I should have explained everything to you, and I should have rung her."

"Arrow," I said, "I can't be your mate."

"Honey, it's too late. You wear my mark."

I touched a palm to the back of my neck. "Is that what you did?"

"I didn't mean to, honest, but I sensed you were mine the moment I sat next to you."

"You did?" I gasped.

"I did. Your scent calls to my wolf."

"My Fae scent?"

"You, your scent. Fae or otherwise. I don't give a damn you're a Fae."

"Why Arrow? Why don't you care?"

"Because you're mine. You'll always be mine." He cupped my cheeks in both hands.

I gulped against the burn in my throat. Arrow was a wolf shifter. I was his mate. My head wouldn't wrap itself around the idea. I couldn't comprehend what this meant for my future. For our future.

"All right, you two, break it up. Let me meet my daughter-in-law," his mom said.

Daughter-in-law?

Arrow stepped aside for the woman at his back and wrapped an arm around my waist. His mom stood, a blanket draped around her similar to a sarong. I saw the family resemblance now the threat in her posture had vanished. She smiled at me, a flash of white teeth.

"I'm so honored to meet you," his mom said.

"Honored?" My eyebrows hit my hair.

"You're my son's mate, of course, I'm honored." She threw her arms around me and hauled me into a maternal hug. "Welcome to the family. Let me introduce you both to Clara and Eloise."

"Hello," Arrow said. "Care to explain, Mom?"

"Ray made a deal with an English pack. We'd exchange two of our males for two of their females."

"Who did he exchange?"

She glanced away. "Lyle and Kirk."

"He sent two of my teammates away without discussing it with me first." Arrow roared and paced the dirt, kicking up stones in his anger.

"Now, Arrow, you realize he's trying to do the best thing for the pack."

"Bullshit, he's trying to play games."

"What games?"

Arrow waved a hand at the two young women who surveyed us. "Let me guess, one of you is for me and the other is for Sledge. Is that why you arrived here first? So, I'd get first pick?"

"Arrow, it doesn't matter now you're mated."

"Like hell, it doesn't. There's still Sledge's future planned out for him. And what about Lyle and Kirk?"

"Lyle and Kirk were happy to go to England and choose from the abundance of female wolf shifters over there. You understand as well as I do their female numbers outweigh ours."

"I still don't like it." Arrow scowled.

I sucked in a breath through clenched teeth. Jealousy churned inside my chest. They meant one of these women for Arrow. If I hadn't come back, would he have chosen one? They'd suit a wolf shifter over me. The sounds of the forest resumed as birds chirped and fluttered from tree to tree. When Arrow's mother hugged me, I'd experienced a connection. She was a piece of him. His family, but as a Fae, I'd never fit in with a wolf shifter pack.

I took a step toward the forest.

"Saoirse, are you all right?" she asked.

I shook my head and took another step.

"I don't belong here," I said.

"You do. You're Arrow's mate." She firmed her lips.

"But I'm a Fae princess." I took another step. "How did you comprehend what I was?"

"Your scent, your white hair with the flower crown, and your indigo-ringed eyes are legendary to Fae royalty." She eased closer to me. "It doesn't matter who you are."

"It does." I backed away. "You wanted to rip out my throat."

"That was before I found out you're Arrow's mate."

"It shouldn't make a difference," I sobbed. "I can't do this. I can't be Arrow's mate. He can have one of them for a mate."

"Sweetheart, but you are. He won't choose another now."

"No." I turned to Arrow who stood still like I'd turned him to stone with my words. "No."

I ran into the forest. I wouldn't outrun the wolves. They were faster than me, and they'd scent me, track me. *How didn't I realize he was an immortal too?* I'd screwed up with royal grandness. My father would... Dia, what would he do? He wouldn't approve. He wouldn't let me live in the mortal realm with a different breed of immortal.

No, he wanted Fae to breed more Fae after the near decimation of our race and causing us to remain in The Summer Court. Before then we'd frequented Earth and had relationships with whoever we desired. Now, our laws were strict to ensure the survival of the Fae race.

I ran faster. Trees whipped my arms, branches tangled my feet and legs trying to trip me. Birds started at my approach and flew into the air showing further evidence of the direction I'd fled. I didn't slow though because I comprehended my actions brought consequences.

I'd sensed Arrow was different. And I was different now too. I'd enjoyed sex with an immortal while in heat. Which could only result in one outcome. One I'd never expected. My legs wobbled as I ran, but I kept running. Kept fleeing the one thought that entered my mind.

I'd had sex with an immortal while in heat.

I couldn't be?

I had to be.

There was no other explanation for the way my heat had dissipated so soon after it started. For the way my body felt different since I'd been with Arrow. How I'd felt changed. Transformed even.

I was pregnant to a wolf shifter.

Pregnant. The one thing I'd avoided for years and now I was. I ought to be distressed, angry, anything but happy. *Dare I admit it?* The knowledge I was pregnant with Arrow's baby made me happy. He'd made me happier in our short time together than I'd been in centuries of life.

How old was Arrow anyway? I'd never asked. If I had, he would have told me. His honesty was always forthcoming. He might not have told me what he was, but he'd always intended to. The concerned expression on his face as he revealed he was a wolf shifter attested to the depths of his guilt. And then the pained twist of his mouth and despair in his eyes as I'd turned and fled told me he feared this. Dreaded being rejected by his mate.

But escaping was what I was good at. For how could I be a wolf shifter's mate?

Sounds resonated behind me of running wolves. He'd catch me in seconds. I didn't stand a chance. This couldn't be happening.

"Leave me alone," I screamed.

A howl was my answer.

"I don't want you. I don't want this," I yelled, hoping he wouldn't scent my lie from this distance.

Another howl.

A branch tripped me, and I fell to my hands and knees. My power rippled, drawing water from the surface of the lake. The lake wasn't far now. If I reached the water before they caught me, I'd slip back through the veil and into The Summer Court. Wolf shifters couldn't pass through. Only Fae magic passed through the veil.

What would happen if I returned to the Summer Court? Would the other Fae realize I was pregnant to a wolf shifter? No one had so far, but I'd avoided everyone except Lorcan and Rian. I couldn't risk it. I wouldn't risk the precious life of our baby in The Summer Court.

A sob burst free.

A golden wolf emerged through the green fernery of the undergrowth. I buried my head in my hands. The wolf's warm wet tongue rasped my cheek, licking my tears until they stopped. Arrow was magnificent in his wolf form, a beast of a wolf, larger than any I'd ever encountered.

"You're beautiful," I said, wrapping my arms around the soft fur of his neck, and burying my face in the thickness of it.

He let me hold him in his wolf form. Arrow didn't shift and take me in his arms as I'd expected. I needed this. The quiet acceptance of him and what we meant to each other. I ran my hand over his back, and he laid on the ground next to me coating me with his wolf presence and warmth.

His panting eased, as did my ragged breathing. Even in his wolf form, our connection was powerful. He may have mated with me without me realizing but a part of me, the long-buried part, comprehended he was mine too.

"Arrow."

He placed a paw on my shoulder and nudged my face with his damp nose.

"I don't believe this can work."

His form shimmered and contorted. The fur rippled in a backward wave into his skin. He rotated his head to the side and the wolf face turned into his masculine human face. Paws turned to hands and his body reclaimed his human shape.

"Liar."

My lips wobbled.

"You want me." He drew me into his arms.

"Aye."

"We'll make this work, Saoirse. I'm your fated mate."

I leaned back and met his gaze. "We'll have to, Arrow. I'm pregnant."

CHAPTER SEVENTEEN
SAOIRSE

H E GRINNED. "HONEY, I know."

"What? How?"

He patted the side of his nose. "Wolf, remember."

I cupped his face between my hands. "You're truly my fated mate?"

"Yes." He dropped his nose into my neck and breathed deep sending shivers along my spine.

"How didn't I realize?"

"You were a little preoccupied with sex." He grinned.

I matched his smile. "Aye, my heat."

"Your scent drove me crazy." He scraped his teeth over my ear and nibbled on my jaw.

"And now?"

Even pregnant and my heat over, I longed for Arrow with every piece of me.

"You still drive me crazy but I don't feel like a savage beast anymore."

I puffed out a laugh. "I liked you savage."

"Honey," he rumbled.

He covered me with his weight, and his heat, pressing me into the soft fernery beneath my back and sending up the fragrance of the freshly crushed eucalyptus leaves.

A scent I'd always associate with Arrow. My fated mate.

"I've dreamed of you for so long," I said. "I can't believe I missed the signs." My hands ran over his shoulders, marveling in the rightness coursing through my palms just from touching him.

The knowledge he was my fated mate filled the unhappy places I'd hidden for so long. He plundered my lips with a kiss that seared my essence to my soul. I slid my hands to his chest as my power surged to my hands wanting to mark him as mine. Then I yanked them back. I couldn't mark him here in the middle of the forest. He'd fall into the Quiet.

I broke the kiss. "Arrow"

He skimmed his hands down my side. "Your hands are glowing."

"Aye, tis my power."

"It feels good." He slid down my body. "You feel good."

With infinite slowness, he eased my dress over my hips and buried his face between my legs. A groan rumbled from his chest and through his lips sending vibrations deep into my damp core.

He lifted his glowing golden eyes and moved on top of me.

"I can't wait any longer," he muttered and slid into my slick folds. A shudder racked both our bodies at the intense connection of two fated mates joining. Knowing we were connected for the rest of time.

In the dirt and leaves, we mated with the enormity of the meaning for the first time. For my first time having a fated mate to love and cherish. The one thing I'd wanted forever. I'd never dared to believe I'd find my fated mate locked away in the Summer Court. Until Arrow claimed me. Made me his. I wanted to make him mine too. To place my Fae mating mark on his chest but the action was more than a bite. He'd fall into the Quiet for who knew how long, and I'd be left without him again. I couldn't do it yet. Let alone here. I slid my hands to his back. Gave myself over to Arrow, gave him every part of me to keep and protect.

The gentle thrusts of his hips hit the perfect spot deep inside me. Everything was right with this mating. Everything was right with every time we'd mated before. And we'd mated before, I'd been too slow to realize every time we'd been intimate we'd been mating. Arrow gathered me into his arms. The strength and care behind the embrace told me he cherished me as much as I would cherish him. We were mates. We'd be each other's for eternity.

Each slide of his hardness inside me drew a gasp of pleasure from my lips. Each thrust of his pelvic bone against my clit made me drag him closer with my hands. Our gazes glued to each other's, watching each flicker of pleasure ripple across our faces with every thrust in and out. My orgasm rippled in cresting waves of rightness as my legs quivered and every nerve ending in my body pulsed with the ecstasy rolling through me. Arrow held me close and buried his face in my hair with a deep inhale. A moment later his lips met mine, and he followed me over the edge while he groaned into my mouth never breaking the connection.

He kissed me down from the heights of pleasure with loving kisses that spoke of our future, and an eternity of intimacy.

After our tender moment, he hoisted me to my feet in a swift movement and brushed the leaves and dirt from my back and hair.

"Let's head back home. You're staying, aren't you?"

Home. I smiled. The word circled my heart with truth. My home. Our home. Our babies' home.

"Aye." I placed my hand in his. "We have a lot to talk about. Are your mom and those women out here?"

"No, I told her to wait at the house."

"Thank the Summer Court, she didn't see us." I let out a relieved breath.

"That's what you're worried about?"

"I'm concerned about plenty of things."

"What?"

"My father." I grimaced.

"He won't approve?"

"Are you kidding? My father has intended for me to choose a Fae mate and conceive the next royal. He'll be livid when he finds out I'm pregnant to a wolf shifter."

"He's intended you to what?" Arrow growled.

"You don't understand." I squeezed his hand in reassurance. "Humans almost wiped the Fae from existence, and it's been imperative to rebuild our species."

"Wasn't that hundreds of years ago?"

"Aye. We've been locked away, safe in the Summer Court since that fatal night, but Fae matings are becoming rare, babies even rarer, and we don't always carry to term."

"You're saying you might lose the baby?" His throat worked on a hard swallow.

"It's a possibility, Arrow. Fae pregnancies are unforeseen how they'll turn out. I believe it is to do with our power and our dwindling spring of life. Or it could be the two Fae powers won't merge into a new Fae. We don't know. And we don't understand what's causing the spring to decline. Everything used to be fine before the Trappers and father locked the veil."

"If the cause is Fae powers not merging, then our baby will be fine. I don't have Fae power to contend with your power. Yours is water, isn't it? I only have shifter power." He wrapped an arm around my waist. "I'll help you find the cause of your spring problem."

"My brothers and sisters and I have been searching for a long time for the cause of the spring and have found nothing." I appreciated his need to help, but how could he help where we'd failed. "As a Fae royal I can control all elements like the Fae King. Although as a female my powers are muted to some extent. My greatest power is over water which makes it even worse that I can't find the reason. I can control water and bend it to my will, but I can't find the problem with the spring." He was right,

I'd spilled my secrets to him. "But how did you realize my power is over water?"

"The rain covering us when we mated. I figured it came from you."

"You comprehended I was a Fae from the moment we met and didn't care?"

"I did. You could be a hideous ogre and I wouldn't care. Although I am grateful, you're stunning and sexy."

I laughed. Lightness surrounded my being with Arrow filling my heart. Even with all the problems of our future facing us, and the unlikelihood of the pregnancy resulting in a baby, we'd face our immortal lives together as mates. Fae mated for life too.

Now I'd have to work up the courage to mark him as mine, but first I needed to talk to him about the process.

He held a branch back for me and I stepped in front of his house. His mom paced the dirt, dressed in slacks and a pretty floral blouse. I recalled wearing an outfit of hers while I'd stayed with Arrow the first time, but those clothes were nothing like the ones she wore. At the time I hadn't considered the range of apparel in the closet, but it made sense now I knew they were wolf shifters. The other young women sat on the hood of her car chatting like they didn't care Arrow had a mate, and I was a Fae.

"Mom," Arrow called.

She spun and raced our way. "I'm so glad you're back safe and sound. Arrow your pager is beeping."

He grasped the small black object she held out and read the message. "I have to go."

"Go?" I asked.

"There's a fire." He lifted his head and scented the air. "Shit, I can scent the smoke now. Mom take Saoirse and the other women to the lake. Keep her and our baby safe."

He rushed into the house.

"Baby?" she screeched, launching birds into startled flight from the trees.

"Aye, baby."

"Oh, my, I'll be a grandma." She beamed. "You've made an old shifter happy, sweetheart."

"You don't mind the baby is half Fae?"

"Mind? No, my initial reaction to your presence was wrong. Some of the older shifters resent the Fae for leaving Earth after killing all those dreadful Trappers. Humans were so fearful of supernatural creatures after that. The rest of us had to go into hiding. I guess my parents passed their old resentment onto me."

"Why did the shifters resent the Fae leaving?"

"Because Fae always held the power to do anything they chose."

"We may have power, but we can't do anything we choose. There are consequences."

Arrow rushed out of the house, dressed in his firefighter's outfit. He dropped a kiss to my forehead and jumped into his vehicle leaving me stunned at his quick exit.

"What are the consequences?" she asked, snapping me out of my longing glance after Arrow.

"Death."

"But we're immortal. Fae are immortal."

"Everything has a way to be killed. Your husband and sons died when they shouldn't have."

It was harsh of me to say but even immortals could die. Fae knew that more than anybody.

Her face lost its color. "Arrow told you about them?"

"Aye, he's very proud of them. Will he be safe out there today?" I turned in the direction his vehicle disappeared.

"Every time he goes out, I pray he will be."

"That's not very comforting." I glowered.

"It's what I can offer. Come, let's head to the lake as Arrow wants."

"But I should go with him."

"And do what, sweetheart?" she asked in her kind motherly voice.

"I can help him with my power." I took a step the way he'd left.

She grabbed my arm in a firm grip. "I can't let you do that when you told me you might die. It's my duty to protect my son's mate and his baby."

"I can protect myself from the fire, I can protect Arrow."

"Who will protect you from the consequences?"

I turned her way and glared. She was as commanding as Arrow with her gold-flecked gaze.

"Fine." I shook her hand from my arm.

"Trust Arrow will come back to you."

"But I've only now found him," I moaned.

"Oh, baby girl." She hugged me in a warm maternal embrace.

Baby girl? I must be older than her by centuries. She appeared to be in her mid-forties, but immortals aged different to humans, she might be at least a century.

I sniffled. "I'm sorry."

"It's okay." She rubbed my back. "Pregnancy hormones are a real bitch."

"I didn't consider them."

"Come, let's walk and talk." She waved the other women over. "Clara, Eloise, there's a fire, we need to head to the lake."

The women ran over to us. I resisted the urge to use my power on them for thinking they could claim Arrow for themselves.

"Hey, I'm Eloise. I haven't heard of Fae in Australia before."

I ran an assessing gaze over her. She appeared young, but with intelligence on her face.

"Where have you heard of them?" I asked.

"My great gran met one in Ireland."

I shuddered. Ireland was where my mother's parents came from and where they'd died burned at the stake. Where Father's parents had died too by the treacherous hands of the Trappers. I didn't want to talk about that night. I followed her into the forest without another word.

His mom led the way through the forest to a concealed path behind the dense foliage. She padded the track with well-practiced ease. I shouldn't be heading to the lake, the lake was the last place I should go. My power to slip through the veil was greatest at the lake. I hoped Arrow and his team would put out the fire swiftly and I wouldn't have to stay there long.

"There's something you should understand about wolf shifters," his mom said.

"What?" I asked.

"We stick together."

"What's your name?"

"Marianne Goldstein."

"I'm Saoirse O'Cleirigh."

She turned around and walked backward a few steps. "You have a pretty name, it suits you."

"Thank you." I brushed my hair over my shoulder flinging a flower to the trail.

"Is the flower crown always in your hair?"

"Aye. It makes it difficult for me to walk amongst humans. Some decades I fit in more than others."

"You've frequented Earth?"

"Oh, aye, I've been coming for a few centuries now." She coughed and spluttered. "How old are you?"

"Three hundred and thirty-four. And you?"

"Seventy-five. Is Arrow aware of your age?"

"No. We've lots to learn about each other."

"You'll have eternity to do it." She smiled and spun back around.

"Marianne?"

"Yes?"

"I might not carry the baby to term. Fae have difficult pregnancies." My bottom lip trembled.

She stopped on the track and spun.

"Does Arrow know?"

I nodded my head and bit my lip.

"What did he say?"

"He said I shouldn't worry because the baby is a half-wolf shifter." I wrapped my arms around my waist.

"You want this baby, don't you?"

"Aye," I said. "More than I ever would have imagined."

"Trust Arrow, he's your mate, he'll take care of your needs." She stroked a hand on my clenched arms. "Besides, wolves are stubborn. I'm sure your baby will be too."

"Stubborn? I haven't seen it."

"Give it time, Saoirse, give it time." She sniggered. "Wait until you meet the rest of the pack, then you'll see stubborn."

Behind us, Clara and Eloise snickered too.

I heaved a breath. The rest of the pack. I was now part of a pack, carrying a new pack member. Would the wolves want to rip my throat out because I was Fae? Or protect me because I carried a future pack member? I wiped my damp palms on my dress, my power rose to the surface with my unease.

The wind swirled, and a strong breeze whipped through the trees carrying the stench of smoke. Marianne's head whipped around. Her lips curled back showing her pointed canines. A low grumble vibrated from her throat.

"The wind's changed." She shoved me in front of her. "Run, Saoirse, run, the fire's headed this way!"

CHAPTER EIGHTEEN
SAOIRSE

*W*HAT IS THE CRAZY *woman, wolf shifter, doing?*

I didn't need to run from a fire, I can put the flames out with a wave of my hands and a surge of my power. She changed into wolf form in a rip of clothes and nipped at my heels as though she realized I planned to stop and fight. I wouldn't take on a wolf. Those teeth were sharp enough to shred my flesh. Not that I considered Arrow's mom would attack me now she understood I was his mate and carrying his baby. But the other two women?

I bolted through the trees, branches slashed at my arms and legs resembling the lashings of a whip. A blur of movement to the side revealed more wolves. The young women had changed into wolves too, but there was more, an entire pack of wolves circled me. They yipped and howled at each other and closed in on me. Solid gray forms on each side kept me heading in the lake's direction.

A wall of heat seared behind us. I peered over my shoulder at the red glow of flames bearing upon us with a speed of unimaginable proportions. A pulsing fear raced through my body and I turned back to the track and ran even faster. This was nothing like Lorcan's fire. The crackle of dry timber popped and hissed. The flames bore down on the forest and everything in it.

Kangaroos bounded past us. Horses fled in a flurry of hooves. I choked on a sob when I almost tripped over a fleeing koala. I wanted to scoop up the fluffy animal and carry it with me, but there was more than one escaping koala. Lizards scuttled through the undergrowth. Every living creature was fleeing the inferno.

The roar and heat of the flames grew closer and closer, catching the slower animals who screamed in pain. My heart clenched and tears threatened to spill. The screams so similar to that horrific night. The night I'd helped rescue my mother and sisters but was too late to save my grandparents. I wouldn't let anyone die when I could stop the fire.

The glistening blue lake called to my power. I lifted my hands drawing the water. Water hurtled toward me, rising, and increasing until a wall of blue towered over our heads, a tsunami so large it would douse the fire. With a clap of my hands, the giant wave dropped from the sky and landed on top of the fire. The force so hard it knocked me and the wolves from our feet.

I jumped up, ready to call forth another wave of water, but the first wave extinguished the crackling fire, leaving behind the burned charred remains of the forest. The trees hissed with the heat and moisture sending plumes of steam from the heated limbs. Branches cracked and fell to the ground with a thundering sound.

The wolves staggered to their feet and nudged me forward until we stood on the open expanse of the lake's edge. I brushed a hand through my singed hair dropping a half-dozen flowers to the scorched earth. The fire was close. Too close. *Was Arrow safe?*

The Fae veil rippled with power. I averted my gaze from the scene of carnage, soot, and blackness, the charred remains of trees and animals. I stared at the shining white-gold veil with the expectation of who'd summoned the curtain, my heart racing with fear and more.

The wolves growled at the glistening haze of the veil and circled me. I braced myself for my father's arrival.

The Fae King stepped through the veil separating the two worlds. A grim look and glowing white-gold sword firm in his hand. His white hair billowed behind him as though caught in a breeze. My father's indigo gaze blazed with rage. The Fae King's white-gold crown of thorns writhed around his head, alive and powerful, and just as angry as him.

"Father." I kneeled

King Fintan drifted across the lake, his flowing golden robes hovering above the surface and giving the impression he walked on water. As Fae King he controlled all the elements and could bend them to his will, such was his power.

"Daughter, what is the meaning of this?"

He pointed his sword at the wolves and to the forest behind, causing them to howl in unison. A long, loud howl the entire forest would hear. *Were they calling Arrow?*

I rose and squared my shoulders.

"I put out a wildfire to save everyone."

"Saoirse, my child," he said lowering his hand and the sword. "You must not perform these powers on Earth. Do you not remember how the humans coveted our powers?"

"I remember," I said.

"Then why would you use them? Risk exposing yourself this way? Why would you even come here?"

"This is my home now, Father. These are my pack members."

Arrow's mom nudged my hand with her nose. I placed a calming hand on her head, but her lips stretched back in a snarl even though no noise escaped.

My father sheathed his sword and folded his arms. "Your home is in The Summer Court."

"My home is here now with my mate."

"You mated to a wolf shifter," he bellowed, making the animals on the shore of the lake scuttle back into the burned forest. He tapped a hand to his forehead and rubbed.

"Father." I stepped toward him. "Don't you wish for your children to be happy? In all my years I've never known happiness as I have with Arrow."

His indigo eyes softened, and he stepped closer to me. The wolves growled.

"Enough." He flicked a hand toward the wolves. "Or do you wish me to set your forest back on fire?"

"Father," I gasped. "You wouldn't."

He shrugged in the way a King with so much power could do, and the wolves ceased their growling.

"Saoirse, come home with me, and I'll forget this ever happened."

"No." I shook my head flinging another singed flower to the ground. "I'm not leaving my mate."

He waved to the forest. "Where is this mate you keep mentioning? If you covet him so, why isn't he by your side?"

"He's a firefighter, he was off fighting the fire."

The Fae King threw his head back and laughed. "And you doused the flames in one wave."

He hugged me then. My father wrapped his arms around me as his breeze coated me, and the power of the elements rushed over me. The Fae King's power was electrifying. My skin itched with the surge in power, and with the way my power responded to his. The sentiment behind his embrace caused a lump to form in my throat. How could I live on Earth and never see my family again?

"Let go of my mate," Arrow growled.

My father laughed again and spun me around in his arms. "What will you do wolf? She's my daughter, mine to protect. If I say she's returning to the Summer Court with me, you cannot stop me."

"But her child is mine and mine to protect."

My father hissed in my ear. "You're pregnant to a wolf too?"

"Aye. I have feelings for him, Father."

"Feelings?" he asked.

"Aye. You can't tell me you don't know what feelings are. You love Mother."

"I forbid this mating in The Summer Court."

"We're not in The Summer Court. Our laws are different on Earth," Arrow said.

"Father," I beseeched. I couldn't let Arrow take on my father, as impressive as he was, he was no match for the power of the Fae King. "T'was not so long ago we lived here too."

"No," he rumbled. "It was not so long ago I don't remember how the humans persecuted and decimated the Fae. I can't let this happen again. I vowed I'd never let anyone harm my family again."

He drew me toward the lake and the shimmering veil, his power so strong it held me in place.

Arrow jumped forward. "No."

The Fae King wielded his power in a gust of wind and threw Arrow backward on the shore. I tensed in his arms.

"Don't hurt him," I begged.

We glided across the lake toward the shimmering veil. Arrow staggered to his feet and ran toward me. The Fae King sent a wave of water over Arrow, then a flash of icy wind. Arrow froze mid-step in a block of ice.

His pained expression was the last thing I saw before we passed through the veil. I fell to my knees on the marble floor in the palace of the Summer Court.

My mate was frozen.

My heart froze along with him.

The prison in the palace's basement was a stark reminder of what I'd lost. Freedom to come and go from the Summer Court. Also, the chance to return to Arrow. The solid gray walls of granite and stone closed in around me like a noose around my neck. Dark and dreary. No water for me to play with. No chance to let my power help me.

I couldn't summon the strength to even try to escape. Escape was futile. Father seemed to have snapped after discovering me on Earth. Mated to a wolf shifter. And pregnant too. Arrow was safer with me here locked away.

A tiny insubstantial sensation trickled into my Fae royal powers.

"I know you're there Ciara," I said from the small cell.

"How?" Ciara moved from the shadows of the gray stone into the light golden sunlight streaming in through the barred window.

"You always hide in the shadows."

"Still doesn't tell me how." She stepped up to the bars in her navy and black attire so suited to her skulking around the palace.

"I'm your big sister, it's my job to look out for you." I smoothed my hands down my wrinkled dress.

She laughed. "How do you think you'll do that while imprisoned?"

"Dia." I sighed. "I've messed up so much."

"How did you mess up, Saoirse?"

I stood from the single sparse bed and shuffled closer to Ciara. "Father hates me."

"Father would never hate you."

I sighed. "I know, but my actions have hurt him."

"Father will get over it in due course." She gripped the bars with her pale fingers.

"I doubt it," I scoffed. "He's furious with me."

"Why? I saw him bring you down here. Tell me why."

I inched closer and wrapped my fingers around the bars next to hers. "You understand I visit Earth looking for the cause of the decline in the Spring Baile, and I also go while I'm in heat."

Ciara nodded. "I don't blame you. It's a viable solution. Being in heat is intense."

"I'm aware. I'd hoped to find a solution to our declining numbers before you fell in heat."

"I'm close to figuring it out." She scratched her nose on the bars. "There are so many books in the library. It's been a chore to find the right ones to read."

"Yet you are finding them. Better than I'm doing trying to find the source of the decline in our Spring Baile. It's no wonder you all hate me."

Ciara gasped and touched my fingers. "We don't hate you. Whatever gave you the impression?"

I shifted away from the barred door and stared through the bars on the window to the perfection of the Summer Court sky of cerulean blue and rolling fluffy white clouds.

"Saoirse I'm sorry if I ever made you feel that way. It was never my intention. Never our brothers and sisters intention. It's been hard for all of us. The Fae are getting restless. Father and Mother are trying to bring hope back to our people by having us choose mates. We're all trying our best to come up with a solution to our problems and failing."

With a sigh, I slumped onto the lumpy mattress and tugged the scratchy material of the blanket around my shoulders.

"I let a wolf shifter mate with me and I'm pregnant. I know you don't hate me, I suppose it's the pregnancy hormones making me irrationally emotional."

She shook the bars with a loud rattle. "You're pregnant? You mated?"

"Aye." A tear slid down my cheek unheeded. "Now I'm imprisoned for it and using my powers to save the wolf pack from a wildfire on Earth."

"Your mate will come for you no matter if he's Fae or not. So long as he wears your mating mark, he'll be able to find you, even here."

Another tear plopped from my cheek. "I didn't mark him."

"Dia," she exclaimed. "Why ever not?"

"At first, I didn't realize what he was, who he was, and what he meant to me. Then when I learned he was my mate, I realized I was pregnant at the same time too. I'm so worried about the baby making it to term. What if I'd marked Arrow and he'd fallen into the Quiet for a long time, and I lost the baby and didn't have him to hold me and comfort me?" I rubbed my stomach. "I've avoided this for so long, and now it's here. I'm scared, Ciara."

"Oh, Saoirse," she choked out. "I wish I could hug you right now."

I sobbed and wiped my face with the rough material of the blanket as the tears wouldn't cease.

"Listen, this Arrow is your mate maybe he'll find a way to you, anyway."

I shook my head. "You comprehend as well as I do there's no way into the Summer Court unless you're Fae. They designed the veil too well and the lock is impossible for anyone without royal blood to open. How else do you think Father kept everyone out for this long?"

"But if we can slip through it..."

"We're his offspring, we have his powers too, albeit a lesser version. It's the reason we can pass through the veil without him detecting us. Your studies would have revealed that."

"They did." She kicked the bars. "There has to be another way."

"There is no other way. Even if Arrow were to come here, Father would never approve of our mating. He'd most probably kill him."

"No," she said. "Even if he weren't Fae, I can't believe Father would kill your mate on purpose."

"I want to believe that too, but you didn't see him when he discovered my indiscretion." I pressed a hand to my forehead. "Father is not himself."

"I'll talk to him. We'll all talk to him."

"I doubt it will do any good. Don't tell the others, please. I don't want them to know how I've failed you all." I laid down on the bed and curled onto my side. "He'll imprison me here for the rest of my life."

"You think Father will keep you here?" She flung her hand around the prison. "How am I meant to keep that from everyone? And Mother? She won't allow you to stay here."

"What else can he do with me? I wear a wolf shifter's mating mark. I carry a wolf shifter baby. He can't let me out." My throat worked on a thick swallow. "What would the other Fae say? They would realize I'd been to Earth. They'd know it was possible for them to go there too. Father still wants to protect everyone by keeping us locked away."

"Who cares what they'd say? They should be allowed to go to Earth if they want." She huffed out a breath. "I don't care you're mated to a wolf shifter. It's cool you found a mate who's another immortal creature."

I snort laughed. "You think it's cool because you've met no other immortal creatures."

She sighed. "I've studied them, but it's not the same. What are they like? Wolf shifters?"

"Intense. Demanding. Controlling. And yet, caring, and gentle." I closed my eyes and recalled Arrow's perfect image. "He's tall and powerful. A body with rippling muscles and strength beyond anything I've encountered. And the way he kissed me like I was the very oxygen he needed to survive."

"Sounds dreamy," Ciara murmured.

"He is." I sighed on a long, drawn-out breath of longing.

"Sounds like you might love him too."

I opened my eyes and sat up. "Love?"

"Well, yes, mates love each other." She gripped the bars again.

"We all appreciate you love your friend Malachi." I placed a hand behind my head and studied my younger sister's reaction.

"I do even if he doesn't realize it. It's hard avoiding him while I'm in heat."

"I applaud your strength to stay away from him."

"My strength is fading." Her gaze dipped to her feet. "I don't want to risk our future babies. If he even wants me that way."

A small smile tugged my lips for I'd always thought Ciara and Malachi were meant for each other. I guess time would tell if I was right.

"Do you think I'll carry to term?" I asked the question that'd been burning a hole inside my head since I'd discovered I was pregnant.

"I don't know, Saoirse. A mixed-breed hasn't happened since we moved permanently to the Summer Court. I'll have to research the library." She spun from the bars. "I'll be back. I'll let you know what I find in the books."

"Thank you," I said.

Alone in the dreary cell, I did the one thing I'd wanted to do since discovering I was pregnant, talk to my baby. And talk I did. I told our baby how much I loved the life growing inside me already, how much Arrow and I wanted to welcome him into the world, how much we couldn't wait to watch him grow and bloom into a life of love and acceptance. I said all the things I didn't want to be lies.

For others might never accept our baby.

If our baby lived.

All I had was the time in my company. Time to ponder the poor decisions I'd made. Decision's which had fetched me to this cell. To Arrow. To this baby.

I wouldn't change one of them.

CHAPTER NINETEEN
ARROW

THE COLD WAS UNBEARABLE, but the cold in my heart was worse when Saoirse was taken by the Fae King. Her father. Back to wherever they originated from. Inside the ice, I couldn't even blink, let alone smash the block of ice to pieces in the way I wanted. If it was real ice and not magical ice, I might have suffocated over and over again just to come back in the way of an immortal. Thankfully small pockets of air filled my lungs and kept me conscious. Made me wonder if the Fae King hadn't been out to kill me but just restrain me.

"Arrow, we've called for a witch to come help, but you appreciate how they are," Mom said.

Shit. Everyone knew witches sold their magic to the highest bidder, and for taking their sweet ass time about helping any other immortal supernatural being.

All the wolves shifted back to their human form and paced the shore.

"We'll get her back for you," Sledge said stopping in front of me. "She saved the pack from the wildfire."

I longed to shake my head, and demand I be the one to retrieve my mate, but Sledge was my best friend, of course, he'd want to help me. Fear laced the cold in my heart, if this was what the Fae King did to his daughter's mate, he wouldn't hesitate to hurt Sledge. Maybe even kill him.

"She's his mate too," Mom said. "And pregnant."

"Way to tell your best friend you're going to be a daddy," Sledge said.

Stupid ice. As if I wouldn't have told Sledge. I'd found out today my mate was pregnant. I hadn't the time to tell anyone. It was dumb luck Mom was there today.

Mom paced in front of me. "How can we go to where they departed?"

"Where did they go?" Sledge asked.

"I don't know. My family despised Fae. I never took the time to learn about them. Someone in the pack must know about them?" She stared at the two women she'd traveled with from England. "Eloise, didn't you say your great grandmother met a Fae?"

Eloise stepped in front of my frozen body.

"I did, and she did."

"Do you know anything about them?" Mom asked.

"Only the stories I've been told. I've never met one before today, and a princess at that," Eloise said.

Like she needed to remind me Saoirse was a princess. It made the Fae King's actions even more despicable he'd force his daughter to leave her mate.

"Well, tell us, child," Mom said.

Eloise spread her hands and said, "Many years ago the Fae lived between the two worlds of the Summer Court and here on Earth helping anyone who needed help and using their powers over nature for the good of all kind. But humans were greedy, and many humans feared the power they wielded. In time, they turned on them." She turned to face them.

"The humans began small. A Fae here, and there, they burned them at the stake believing fire would release the Fae's powers and transfer them to themselves. The Trappers as they were known became frustrated when it didn't work. They captured and burned more and more Fae at the stake. They even killed the Fae King and Queen. The new Fae King and his army retaliated and destroyed every last Trapper. He gathered up the remaining Fae and left Earth for the safety of the Summer Court where he sealed them in. To this day, that is where they remain hidden and safe from humans."

Eloise huffed out a breath after her long speech.

With each word, she spoke my heart sank a little further into the icy dread. There would be no way her father would approve of our mating. No way he'd let his daughter live on Earth. He doomed me to a life without my mate. Without my child, if it survived. The baby would survive. Our child was part wolf shifter, and stubborn, it wouldn't die.

"Well, isn't this interesting?" A woman with long black hair and a bright streak of red from her temple to her waist stepped in front of me.

Who was she?

"Pepper, thanks for coming on such short notice," Sledge said. "Can you help my friend?"

Sledge knew a witch by her name?

She placed a hand on the ice and studied every angle of my frozen body.

"The power behind this is strong. Lucky for you I have an affinity to fire. It'll cost you."

"Name your price," Sledge said.

She cackled. Seriously, cackled like a damn witch in a movie.

"My price, dear Sledge, is a thousand dollars and a favor from you to be called upon any time I wish."

"Deal," Sledge agreed.

No. I screamed inside my head since the ice had frozen my mouth shut.

They shook hands on their deal. *What did Sledge do?* Owing a favor to a witch was bad, terrible. Everyone knew they were crafty and didn't care about anyone but themselves.

Pepper twirled her hand over the ice and murmured under her breath. An instant warmth transferred from her glowing orange hand into the block of ice. Bit by bit she melted the ice. Bit by bit my body twitched and shifted until I was free from the arctic cold. I fell to the wet, soot-covered dirt, every inch of my body ached from being encased in ice.

"Thank you." My teeth chattered.

Mom wrapped a blanket around my shoulders. I shrugged it off.

"How do I get to the Summer Court?" I demanded.

She cackled. "You don't."

"But I need to get my mate back."

Pepper kneeled in front of me and ripped open my shirt. Her gaze flickered over every inch of my skin in a methodical, almost medical way.

"What the fuck?" Sledge roared.

I stilled him with a hand.

"What is it?" I asked.

"I'd hoped for a second there." She shook her head. "There's no way to cross the veil separating Earth from the Summer Court unless you're a Fae or marked as a Fae's mate."

"She's my mate." I shoved up onto my knees.

"She may be your mate," Pepper said. "You may have marked her in your wolf shifter way, but she hasn't marked you as her mate."

I fell back on my ass. "Fae mark their mates."

"Oh, yes, we all have our ways of marking our mates."

"And if she'd marked me?"

"You could have used your mate connection to pass through the veil yourself."

The blows kept on coming with Saoirse. If she'd marked me as her mate, I could rush into the Summer Court and rescue her. Like a damn prince. Fuck, she was a princess. And I was nothing but a firefighter wolf shifter.

Double fuck.

Saoirse mustn't have marked me on purpose. She'd have known I could go with her to the Summer Court.

Saoirse didn't want me for her mate. As much as her coming back to Earth meant to me, it wasn't what she wanted. If she did, she would have claimed me.

I lifted my head and howled to the sky.

"Never mind, lover," Pepper said. "One wolf shifter over there will be happy to help you get over the loss of your mate."

I didn't even spare Eloise and Clara a look. I wasn't interested in anyone except my mate Saoirse. Except she didn't want me. She didn't mark me.

It stung. Stung like a burn on my flesh.

"Not interested," I ground out.

"Well, then." Pepper patted my knee. "You'll have to hope she comes back."

I glared at the stillness of the lake knowing I'd hope all right. I'd wish Saoirse returned to me. If she did, shit, if she convinced her father the freaking Fae King to let her leave the Summer Court for Earth and her wolf shifter mate, then a miracle would have happened.

There was no way Saoirse would be back.

Weeks later my wolf was still furious. I was furious. I left the mess of clothes and dishes in my once neat and tidy house in my wolf form and paced the shore of the lake. The gentle lap of the water reminded me of Saoirse and her love of water. Of the way she'd smell like the freshest rain on Earth. Except she was no longer on Earth. She was in another place. A place I couldn't go.

Because she didn't mark me.

It smarted.

I threw back my head and howled to the twilight of the evening sky.

"Quit your howling, wolfie," the witch said.

I lifted my gums to show my teeth.

Pepper placed her hands on her hips. "You asked me to come here and you're giving me lip?"

With great effort and a tug of wills to change, I relinquished my wolf form. The wolf believed he'd find Saoirse, and he'd fetch his mate home. I shucked on my pants I'd left lying on a log before changing this morning and pacing the shore. It'd become a daily ritual.

Pacing. Watching. Waiting for Saoirse.

She never returned home though.

"I asked you to come days ago." I yanked a black t-shirt over my head.

"Yeah, well, I'm a busy witch and I already told you I can't help."

"Please, there has to be something you can do?"

I wasn't above begging to get my mate back.

She shook her head. "The Fae King's powers are too strong to penetrate."

"But you unfroze me." I shoved my hands in my pockets, not wanting to remember the cold and the tormenting emotions of the moment Saoirse disappeared.

"Ah, yes." She paced away to the very edge of the lake. "I'm good with fire, and that's what you needed, plus his powers didn't hold you there, it was the ice." She lifted both hands and held them out in front of her. "This is different."

"What's different?"

"Come here. Your wolf picks up on the vibrations of the veil. It's why he paces here."

I shuffled to stand beside her. "What veil?"

She grabbed my hand and held it palm up to the lake. "Why, the veil separating our two realms of course. Close your eyes and you might sense it."

I dropped my lids shut. The sounds of the forest grew louder, the splash of the water on the shore more intense, the scent of the water, the forest, and the witch beside me grew until my nose itched. My wolf bristled. The witch's hand burned hotly, but around her hand, there was a current.

"I sense something."

"That is raw power you can sense. No one can wield power that deep to force a sealed barrier between worlds other than a king."

I snapped my eyes open. "So, we find another king to undo it."

Pepper laughed. "There is no other king beside the Fae king who can unlock the veil."

"We have an Alpha."

"Not the same." She dropped my hand.

"You witches have...?"

"Wouldn't you like to know?" She flung her hair over her shoulders. "Other shifters have leaders. Vampires have a master, ghouls have a queen, angels have God, demons have their king, the sirens have a king but the queen is the one with the power, the elves have a king but I wouldn't venture there. But they all possess different powers to the Fae. You get the point."

"Only the Fae King can break the Fae barrier."

"Spot on. Now I've wasted enough time. Pay up."

I wrenched my wallet out of my back pocket and handed her a wad of cash. She counted the notes with a quick flick of her fingers before stuffing the cash down her jade green top and into her bra.

"But how did Saoirse go through the barrier by herself?"

"Only the king and his descendants would be able to go through it when it's this tightly sealed."

I sighed. "She's his daughter."

"A princess. Nice." She grinned. "Well, if she came through the barrier once, she'll come through again."

"I'm not so sure," I muttered lifting my hand and skimming the air, but without the witch's help, I lost the sensation.

As I lost Saoirse.

"If you need help with anything else, don't hesitate to pay for my services," Pepper said.

I scoffed. She hadn't helped today. *Why would I pay her again? What was the point of everyone being powerful but unable to do the one thing I needed?*

Pepper left me to my sulking. Once the trees stopped rustling with her departure, I shed my clothes and let my wolf howl his pain to the moon hanging low in the darkening sky.

CHAPTER TWENTY
SAOIRSE

T HE SUN ROSE AND set multiple times. The gloomy shadows from the bars on the window were the only thing to change each day. Ciara visited every day with food and water, she didn't stay long, she had too much studying to get through, what with looking for a cure for the deterioration in the Spring Baile and looking into past Fae wolf shifter mating's and their progeny.

So far, she'd found no mention of half breeds in the leather-bound books of the grand library in the palace, but as one of the oldest siblings, I remembered a time when Fae's mated with anyone. Some of Mother's family members had been mated to several creatures. After the burnings and our seclusion, we became purebred.

Not one of my other brothers and sisters visited me, but then I'd asked Ciara not to mention my imprisonment to any of them. The only reason she appeared was that she'd witnessed Father drag me down to the dungeon. Ciara assured me she discussed me with

Father every day, but he wouldn't budge on his stance to keep me imprisoned. And Mother still thought I was hiding the mark on my neck from Father so she was unaware I was locked away. It wouldn't be too much longer though before my family came looking for me. There were only so many places in the Summer Court one could hide. We'd all needed time alone at one time or another.

The baby in my body grew over the time. The connection we developed grew too. He was the only one I could talk to besides Ciara. I knew with certainty the baby was a boy. A boy I hoped looked like his father. A boy I hoped would one day meet his father and know the love of his father.

I wanted that for both of us.

A teeny tiny bump protruded from my stomach, imperceptible to anyone but me.

It was a miracle the pregnancy progressed this far.

"Saoirse?"

"Lorcan, what took you so long?"

His hands clenched into fists at his side.

"I didn't realize you were in the prison. I was on Earth looking for you."

"You were?" I walked from the window to the door of the cell.

"Father and I have had some doozy fights. He wouldn't tell me anything."

"You fought Father?"

"I did. Many times." He stepped out of the shadows looming in the dungeon's interior and up to the cell door.

I gasped. "Lorcan, your face."

A bright purple bruise surrounded Lorcan's left eye and radiated in a downward blotch to his cheek and his fat lip still welling with blood.

"It'll heal shortly or when I get to the Spring." He yanked on the door. "First, I'm getting you out of here."

"Lorcan, stop."

Lorcan's hands lit on fire in a blazing red-orange glow. He placed them on the lock until the dark gray bars melted into a puddle at our feet on the cobblestones. The door swung open.

"Come on, let's get you out of here." Lorcan held out his hand now minus the glowing flames.

I shook my head. "Lorcan, no. I can't escape. Father knows where Arrow lives."

"Arrow? Who's Arrow?"

"My mate."

"You can't stay here." He glared at the cell, a curve of his top lip showing his disgust. "I can't believe Father put you here."

A sad smile escaped me. "I didn't give him much choice. I don't want to be here, but if I escape, it'll be worse."

He rubbed the back of his neck. "I don't want you in prison."

"I don't want to be in prison, Lorcan, but I mated with a wolf shifter." I hugged my arms around my middle.

"Is that all?" He shrugged. "Fae used to mate with shifters all the time."

"I remember. It was a long time ago."

"I used to shag shifters before the burnings. Father didn't have a problem with it then."

"He does now." I scowled.

"Screw him. If you're mated, then that's what's important. He can't stand between a mating bond. It's a bigger law than him."

"But what if he hurts Arrow?" I asked through the fear in my throat.

"He won't," Lorcan stated.

"You're so sure."

"I am. Come on, Saoirse, trust me." He shook his hand.

"I've always trusted you." I placed my hand in his.

"Where's your mate? Is he in a cell?" Lorcan glanced down the hallway at the other cells.

"He's not here. He's back on Earth."

"Why isn't he here? The mating bond draws you to each other."

"I haven't marked him." I hung my head.

"Saoirse," he tutted. "Suck up your fear and go get your mate."

"But I don't want to hurt him."

"You're hurting him more by not marking him as yours."

"And you understand this how?" I asked.

We climbed the spiral stone stairs from the dungeon to the lower floor of the palace.

"Because I'm the smartest."

I laughed for the first time in a long time. "Ciara would fight you for the title."

"She might try. She's book smart, but I'm street smart. It's a whole other level of smartness."

"And Briana would think she's smarter than you. Rian too. Aislinn would fight you for the fun of it. Roisin would be the one who'd let you give yourself the title."

"What about you?"

I squeezed his hand. "You've always been the one I look up to."

He laughed. "But I'm younger than you."

"I know."

We snuck down the marble hallway toward the atrium and my chance of crossing through the veil at the Spring Baile since I still couldn't figure out how Rian had cracked the lock by the lake.

"Where do you two think you are going?" The Fae King boomed.

We froze and faced our father.

"I'm leaving," I said.

"I forbid it." Father folded his arms over his chest. His thorn crown wreathed around his white hair.

Lorcan opened his mouth.

The Fae King waved his power at Lorcan and shut his mouth.

"Leave us, Lorcan." He thrust Lorcan from the hallway using his power in a burst of wind.

Lorcan's hands blazed to life in a red-hot flaming fire. Father encased them in ice with quick succession. Lorcan thawed them with his fire and strode in our direction. The Fae King lifted his hands as a flare of his fire of blue-gold flames licked his palms.

"Father, Lorcan, stop. This is my battle."

The pair stopped and stared at me. Father narrowed his angry indigo eyes and waved a hand in Lorcan's direction dismissing him. Lorcan stormed away in a huff down the marble hallways.

"Very well, daughter of mine, we shall spar for your freedom."

"Not what I meant, but if this is what it takes for me and my baby to leave, then I'll spar with you, Father."

His eyes glittered in triumph. Not once in my life had I bested my father in a fight. Not one time had I ever got the upper hand over his immense powers, but I had a lot to fight for. I possessed a mate and a baby. A new life waited for me.

I might even have the chance to love Arrow.

"After you." He waved his hand. "We'll battle in the courtyard."

"Aye, Father." I dipped my head.

Our last wager ended with him as the victor, but today there was too much at stake for me to lose. I'd protect the growing baby inside me with the feral ferociousness of a wild beast. My father didn't comprehend what he had coming to him.

I strode along the hallway, my power growing more with each step the closer we drew to the courtyard. My limbs tingled in anticipation of the battle ahead. The marble hallway gave way to the great columns leading to the courtyard. We stepped underneath the crystalline structure and into the open air. I inhaled a calming breath.

"We can end this now, and you can go back to your cell," he offered.

"No, you can't keep me locked up forever, Father. What will you say to Mother? To my brothers and sisters? Do you think they'd let you keep me in prison all because I mated with a wolf shifter?"

"T'was more than you mating with a wolf shifter. You broke through the locked veil. You visited Earth. You placed all the Fae here in jeopardy by using your powers to help humans."

"I was trying to help us. I went to Earth looking for a cure to our spring," I said. "I helped where we once used to help Earth."

"After everything the humans done to us, you would help them?"

"You vanquished the Trappers. Those humans are innocent of their crimes." I widened my stance and called a water sword to my hand.

He lifted an eyebrow. "Katana? Do you think the samurai sword will help you win this fight?"

"I didn't waste my time in Japan gazing at the flowering cherry trees, Father." I swung the sword.

He called a matching sword to his hand and blocked my blow. I stepped back, not a moment too soon. Father swung at my face. The water sword swished in his hand. On my next upswing, he grabbed my elbow. I thrust forward and shoved him off me. He lunged forward and swung an almighty swipe of his sword. I lifted my Katana to stop the blow from hitting my chest. Our eyes met for the beat of heart.

I rushed back three paces and gave myself more room for his next attack. He lunged forward again. I blocked with my sword swiping up over my head. Swinging my arm crashing down on his arm I punched him in the chest. To his shock and mine, he staggered back a hand clutched to his chest.

I lifted my Katana sword. He lifted his. We stared at each other.

"Oh, my precious daughter," he murmured.

His words hurt my heart.

He rushed toward me. Our swords clashed in front of us, a blaze of shining water blades reverberating against each other in repeated swings. Swing, block, swing. He ducked and rolled. I slashed with my Katana. The long blade of the sword caught his cheek. A slash of red welled to the surface. His cheek twitched and healed leaving behind a stripe of blood.

From his knees, he said, "You want to leave the Summer Court?"

"I'll always want to come here."

"Then why fight me on this?" he asked sounding exasperated.

"Because we can have both."

"We did once and we almost lost everyone because of it," he seethed.

He lunged. A swish of his sword in the air. I stepped backward in a hurry.

"You want to leave your family too?" His voice came out thick with emotion.

"No." I blocked his blow. "I want Arrow and my baby to be a part of this family."

"You can't have it both ways."

Our swords clanged in the air then met in the middle, locked together.

"Why not?" I asked.

He shoved me back. I flipped in the air, feet flying over my head, my hand landed on the ground as my sword struck at his legs.

The Fae King grunted and staggered to the side. He swung to hit me. I protected the baby and blocked him as a thud of sword on sword vibrated up my arm. Every feeling I held for the baby and Arrow surged through my blood and roared in my ears. I slashed my sword across his stomach. He flinched back, but I was too fast for once in my hundreds of years. Blood sprayed his robes. My father collapsed to his knees.

"Father," I cried, calling my water Katana to disintegrate, I rushed over to kneel in front of him.

"You won." His sword clattered to the parquetry floor. His hands clutched his stomach as bright red blood pooled at our knees.

"I didn't mean to hurt you." I pressed my hands against the gushing flow of blood as tears stung the backs of my eyes.

"Use your power," he rasped out in pain-filled words.

I summoned my power over water. Drawing on the Spring Baile a gush surged through the air in a stream and reached my side. I gathered the water in my hands and bathed the long gaping wound. The skin sealed together in measured increments until a pink line lay across his stomach leaving no trace of the catastrophic injury I'd caused my father.

Red blood coated both our hands and clothes. I swallowed in fear and regret I'd grievously injured my father in my quest to leave the Summer Court. He was my father, and I loved him, including his flaws.

"Let me help you to the spring." I tugged on his arm urgently even though his wound was almost healed.

He lifted his head and cupped my face with his bloody hand. "You've always been the child to surprise me the most."

"I have?"

"Yes, Saoirse. I may not have said it until now. I'm proud of you." His eyes glistened. "I've always kept you safe."

"You have, but you've trained me well. I can keep myself safe." I covered his bloody hand with mine. "Let me go to Earth. My life is with my mate now."

"I cannot imagine a life without you in it." He fell onto his back.

"Mother!" I screamed. No, no, he was almost healed. There couldn't be anything wrong with the great Fae King.

There was only one person who could help my father, his mate, the Fae Queen.

"Mother!"

Hurried footsteps echoed through the grand halls of the palace. Mother's calming presence washed over me before she kneeled beside me. She sang soft lulling words in a soothing chant. A golden glow emanated from my father. His stomach smoothed to its once-unmarked form. My mother was the most phenomenal Fae Queen to ever rule with her power filled singing voice.

I choked on a sob.

Mother gathered Father into her arms singing the entire time. He wrapped his arms around her neck and nuzzled into her hair. A golden glow covered them with the power of their mating bond.

I rocked back on my bottom and hugged my knees to my chest. In my quest for my freedom, I'd injured my father. I was the worst daughter ever.

He lifted his head, gazed into the eyes of his mate then turned to me. "If you wish to return to Earth, I can't have you come back here and risk the humans finding us. You can go to your mate now, I won't stop you from having what I share with your mother."

Mother leaned down and pressed her lips to his in a sweet claiming kiss. A kiss I'd seen many times over the years. Their love was epic. A love I longed for with my mate.

"I understand, but times have changed, Father, it's time we changed with them. It's time you unlocked the veil."

"Perhaps one day." He swallowed as his eyes glistened. "I keep trying my hardest to protect you all and I keep failing each one of you miserably."

I sucked in a shocked gasp. "You're not failing." Tears gathered in my eyes and spilled down my cheeks. I clasped his hand. "I love you, Father."

"I love you too, Saoirse," he croaked out and squeezed my hand

The love and affection I held for my father flowed from me. He wasn't the worst father in history. He'd overreacted to finding me on Earth. After everything he'd endured, it was no wonder he was fearful of my safety.

I stood in a flourish and ripple of power longing to reunite with my mate.

All I could do now was hope my family would come to find me on Earth one day. One day he'd remove the lock on the veil and we'd travel freely between the two realms. I knew for a fact Lorcan would come, our closeness guaranteed he'd search for me. I longed for the day he would arrive, and I'd embrace my favorite sibling again. For now, I'd have to do with embracing my mate.

My power crackled with energy, I'd never felt stronger in my life. The veil between the two worlds shimmered right in front of me. Rian's words drifted back to me. We didn't need the Spring to call the veil, we possessed the power inside ourselves. My oldest brother was right. Power like nothing I'd ever used before swirled greater. The call of my fated mate made me powerful beyond comprehension.

Mother stopped singing and stood to embrace me in a long hug. "Saoirse, my beautiful princess, please stay safe. I love you. We all love you." Tears streamed down her cheeks. "Be happy with your mate as I have been with mine." She kissed my damp cheeks. "I will miss you more than words can say."

"I love you, Mother. I'll miss you too," I struggled to say through the emotions clogging my throat.

She gave me a sad smile. "Now I know how my mother felt when I left Earth to live in the Summer Court."

Tears spilled from my eyes. I'd miss her. I'd miss them all, but my future was with my mate and our child. We released each other and she returned to Father's side.

She sobbed so hard her shoulders shook. Father gathered her closer.

I stepped through the shimmering indigo blue veil and left the Summer Court for the exact location of Arrow outside The Pup's Tavern. I chuckled. The name of the tavern made sense now I understood the people in Crystal Creek were wolf shifters. I patted my stomach. I would have a pup soon too.

"Let's see your Dad," I said to the baby.

CHAPTER TWENTY-ONE
ARROW

I NURSED THE COLD beer bottle between my unfeeling hands inside the tavern. Nothing appealed to me these days. Not beer. Not the two wolf shifter women vying for mine and Sledge's attention. Eloise, or was it Clara, rubbed her hand up and down my back in what she meant to be a soothing gesture, but was more her hand feeling me up in a way I didn't like.

"Don't," I mumbled.

The ache inside me wouldn't go away. My wolf whimpered, a constant reminder of how I'd lost our mate. He didn't need to remind me how upset he was. I was upset too. The woman's hand ventured lower.

"I have a mate," I growled.

My wolf rumbled. My nails sharpened around the beer bottle and clicked on the glass. A scent twitched his nose. Fuck how he remembered the sweet scent of his mate. The wildness of her spring rain and the way she'd coated our mouths with the taste of her.

A gust of wind blew the tavern door open. I started at the sudden cool breeze blowing through the room and raised my head to the door.

Saoirse stood there, a blood-soaked hallucination.

I lifted my drink to my lips finishing the cold liquid in one swallow. At least the alcohol was real. At least I'd fall into a dreamless sleep tonight with the amount of booze I'd drunk during the day and night. Images of Saoirse wouldn't haunt my mind.

She drifted across the dark timber floor of the tavern dressed in a pink dress marred with the splatter of red. More red splatters were smeared across her tear-stained cheeks. Her blonde hair was tipped with the same blood-red. All sound stopped. The only noise I caught was the thud of my heart in my ears.

"Arrow," she said.

I blinked. The alcohol hazed my hurting head. Made it swim and spin as I slumped on the stool. She couldn't be real. Or was she?

Eloise or Clara shifted closer to me and said, "He's mine now."

I'd already told her I would never be hers. I was Saoirse's mate. Even if she didn't want me.

"Get your hands off my mate," Saoirse said.

"You haven't marked him as yours," the woman said.

"He. Marked. Me," Saoirse ground out through clenched teeth.

I shrugged out of the woman's hold. Her arm left my back. Relief surged through me to no longer experience her unwanted touch.

A scuffle broke out between Saoirse and what was her name?

But every cell of my body was frozen in shock. Saoirse was here. Truly here?

"Dude, what's wrong with you." Sledge grabbed me by the collar of my shirt, hauled me off the stool and punched me in the face. "Snap out of it."

A loud crack exploded in my ears as pain radiated across my jaw.

"What the fuck," I growled and rubbed my aching face.

The haze of alcohol and shock of seeing Saoirse lifted with the pain. The scent of blood drifted to my nostrils. Two, no three sets of blood. Two Fae, one wolf. Saoirse's blood. Who dared make my mate bleed? I swung my head in the scent's direction. A roaring growl exploded from my chest. I landed on my paws in a flurry of tearing clothes and transforming fur and bones.

I attacked the wolf in a burst of speed and strength, of teeth and claws ripping at fur and flesh. *How dare she attack my mate?* My pregnant mate. We tumbled on the wooden floor of the bar as all my frustration manifested onto the woman who hadn't taken no for an answer. Her paws scrambled for purchase to escape me, but I knocked her over with a solid thump of my body into hers. The wolf rolled on the floor whining with her tail tucked between her legs. I stood over her and snarled, showing her my teeth. Eloise whimpered again.

"Stay away from my mate," Saoirse growled sounding like a wolf shifter herself.

Eloise scampered from the tavern in her wolf form through the open door. Sledge slammed the door shut behind her and folded his arms.

The townspeople in the bar were silent. I stalked to Saoirse.

"Arrow?"

A rumbled filled my chest. She'd called me her mate, but she hadn't marked me as hers. There was only one reason she'd do that. And that was if she didn't want to claim me.

She dropped to her knees and held her hands out to me. My lip curled back even as I hungered to go to her.

"You don't frighten me." She dropped her arms. "What's wrong?"

I paced away from her and back again. My wolf raged at me to drag her away and force her to submit to me. I battled the wolf. She didn't want me. If she did, she would have put her Fae mating mark on me.

Sledge cleared his throat and stepped forward.

I snarled at Sledge.

He held up his hands. "Dude, I'm your best friend, I wouldn't hurt your mate."

I sat on my haunches.

Saoirse turned to Sledge. "What's wrong with him? I've only seen his wolf once and he wasn't like this. Is this normal?"

"Arrow discovered that Fae mark their mates, and you didn't mark him, so he's being a douche and thinks you don't want him," Sledge said.

"Ah." She crawled across the floor to my side. "There's a reason I didn't mark you yet, Arrow." She tentatively stroked my back. "Won't you shift back so we can talk this through?"

I huffed even though her touch had grounded me in an instant. I shifted losing the soothing comfort of her palm. Angus threw me a pair of gray tracksuit pants over the bar. I slid them on and stood.

"Saoirse, you're really here?"

"Aye," she said standing with me.

"I never thought I'd see you again." I lifted a hand and dropped it, afraid if I touched her, she'd disappear again. "You're injured."

"It's nothing." She rubbed a hand across the scratch on her arm and wiped the blood away.

I lifted her arm and tested the small cut with a swipe of my thumb. The wound wasn't bad. A slight scratch from a wolf shifter's claw already healing on her Fae skin. I swung my gaze at the door. Eloise wouldn't dare come near my mate again. I'd make sure of that. My nose twitched with the aroma of mixed blood coming off her.

"Whose else's blood are you wearing?"

"My father's." She grimaced and tugged her arm from my grip. "I fought him and injured him to return to you."

I tilted my head and studied the dried red blood of a handprint on her cheek.

"But you don't want me for your mate."

"I never said that," she exclaimed.

"You should've stayed in the Summer Court." I sat on a stool at the bar, a rejected slump dropping my shoulders.

"Arrow you can't mean that." She slid onto the stool beside me.

Sledge walked across the tavern to join the other townspeople watching our show. I didn't want to do this here with her, but if we were alone, she'd tempt me to believe anything she said, tempt me to lose myself in the welcoming heat of her body.

"Why are you here, Saoirse?" I heaved out a breath. Because having her here and having her leave me again would break me. I wouldn't survive a third time.

She swallowed. "Because you're my mate."

"If I'm your mate, wouldn't you have marked me?"

"Oh, Arrow." She grabbed my hand and leaned forward. "I want to, I wanted to the moment I realized we were fated mates, but I don't want to subject you to the pain of a Fae mating mark."

"You accepted my mark."

She touched her other hand to her neck and blushed. "I did, and I loved every second, but a Fae mating mark is more than a bite."

"Go on." I squeezed her fingers.

"When I mark you, I'll mark you with my power. It'll thread its way through your entire body. It'll weave an unbreakable connection between us. In the moment of marking you, you'll have access to all my memories."

"All your memories, huh?" My lips spread into a smirk at the idea of learning every passing moment in my mate's life. It appealed so much. She'd kept her past a secret and while I understood her need to do so, I also wanted her to trust me with her secrets. If she marked me, then she'd show me she trusted me. Trusted this fated mating.

"Aye. My mark won't be pleasant. It'll be painful. So painful you'll slip into the Quiet to absorb all the information overloaded in your brain."

"The Quiet? What's that?" I drummed my fingers on the well-worn bar top.

She scanned the room, before settling back on my face. "It's similar to what humans call a coma."

"Huh." I sat back and searched her face. I detected no lies in her scent. Nothing but truth rang from her. "So, when you mark me I'll slip into a coma. For how long?"

"I don't know." She chewed her lip. "I've seen the Quiet last anywhere from a few hours to a few years."

I stood in a rush. The stool screeched across the timber floor. I paced the room. Holy fuck. If I let my mate mark me, then I might be out of action for years. I might miss the birth of our child. No wonder she was hesitant to do it. With a frustrated howl, I swung back to Saoirse and stormed across the tavern to swoop her up into my arms.

"I'm sorry I didn't give you a chance to explain before jumping to the wrong idea."

"I'll always want you as my mate, Arrow. Never doubt that."

She melted into me and wrapped her arms around my neck. The slight bump in her stomach bulged between us. I released Saoirse to stare in wonder at our growing baby. With a tremble in my hand, I placed my palm over her stomach.

"It's a boy," she said.

I lifted my gaze to her face.

"How do you know?"

"I had no one to talk to while imprisoned except the baby. We formed a bond."

"A boy," I said in wonder. "Is he healthy?"

"So far so good." She placed her hand on top of mine. "He's happy we're together. Are you?"

I cupped her bloody face in my hands and kissed her. She didn't need my words, she needed my actions. Saoirse sighed into my mouth and tangled her tongue with mine. I broke the kiss regretting we were in the crowded tavern.

"I'm over the freaking moon with happiness. Mark me, Saoirse. I want the world to know I'm yours."

"Are you sure?" She chewed her lip.

"I'm sure I'm yours as much as I'm sure you're mine."

Tears welled in her eyes.

"What's wrong?" I stroked her bloody, tear-stained cheeks with my thumbs.

"I'll miss you while you're in the Quiet," she said with so much emotion I didn't doubt she wanted this. Wanted me.

"I promise I won't stay there long." My hand brushed down her back. "I have a mate to take home and pleasure."

"Okay, Arrow, let's go home and I'll mark you."

"Do it now, Saoirse. I don't want to wait a second longer. Learning I couldn't go where you lived without your mark was torture. I never want to feel that way again."

Saoirse lifted her hands. She smiled, heat blazing in her eyes. I couldn't wait to take her home and show my mate how much I'd missed her. She ran both hands across my stomach and licked her lips.

"Honey, you keep that up and I'll throw you over the bar."

Saoirse gazed at the bar. "I'd love that."

I groaned. "I'll organize it with Angus for another day."

She laughed huskily and slid her hands up my bare chest. Her palms grew warmer and glowed a luminous silver-pink.

"I'm sorry," she said.

"It's okay. I want this."

"You say that now." She grimaced. Her palms grew warmer still.

I shifted under the growing heat.

"Hold still, Arrow." She dropped her gaze to her hands on my chest.

A surge of pain jolted through every vein in my body. "Shit."

"Sledge," Saoirse said. "Be ready to catch him."

Catch me?

The pain intensified. My knees wobbled. Saoirse stepped closer and flattened her hot glowing palms deeper into my chest. So deep it felt like she forced them into skin and bone straight to my heart. I ground my teeth and held myself still.

Saoirse's eyes drifted shut. Tears fell from her closed lashes. I wanted to lift a hand to her face and brush them away, but my body hurt too much to move. *Was this hurting her too? Why didn't she say it'd hurt her as well?* I never would've agreed to anything that caused her pain.

I opened my mouth to tell her to stop. To not hurt herself for me, but a howl ripped from my burning chest.

My wolf writhed in pain. Unlike the pain from losing Saoirse, this pain grew and grew until my eyes shut and my head pounded to the point it might explode.

"Almost finished," Saoirse said, her voice low.

Her voice echoed through the pain.

Saoirse's hot palms vanished, but the pain continued higher and hotter. Longer and louder than before. Glimpses of scenes I'd never witnessed before shuffled through my head. A world of beauty. A spring of running water. Of a family of brothers and sisters. Faces and feelings that weren't mine embedded themselves in my mind. I clutched my head and moaned.

"I'm sorry, Arrow," she muttered again.

More images embedded themselves making it impossible to answer. Horrifying images. Ashes from human-built fires. Screaming. Burning flesh. Pain. So much pain.

"Make it stop," I cried.

"It's too late," she said. "You need to see all my memories. You need to accept them and all of me for my mark to work."

"Fuck, Saoirse, I can see your family burning."

"It'll be over soon, I promise."

"I, ah, I don't feel good." I opened my eyes, but all I saw was blackness and the images still racing inside my mind.

"Now, Sledge," she said.

The blackness took me over and in the Quiet, Saoirse's long life flashed through my mind.

CHAPTER TWENTY-TWO

SAOIRSE

"**C**AREFUL, SLEDGE," I SAID holding Arrow's front door open.

"It's like carrying the dead weight of a whale," Sledge said, knocking Arrow's feet into the doorjamb.

"Or a wolf," I said.

"He's not dead, is he?"

"No. You can see his chest moving," I reaffirmed for the thousandth time. "He's in the Quiet."

Sledge dropped Arrow's motionless body on his bed. I fussed around my mate, draping a blanket over his legs and drawing it up to his chin. A loud pounding knock echoed through the house from the front door.

"I'll get it," Sledge said.

I nodded and stood guard over Arrow's body. My mate was defenseless while in this state and I'd do anything to protect him considering it was my doing he couldn't defend himself.

Sledge returned with another man.

A water sword formed in my hand before they stepped inside the door of the bedroom.

"Stay back." I spread my legs and bunched the toes of my feet ready to strike.

"Easy, Saoirse." Sledge held up his hands. "This is my dad, Ray Braidwood, the Alpha of the Crystal Creek wolf pack."

I dipped my head and studied the Alpha. He was as large as Sledge with a similar muscular mass, but I could take him with my water sword if the resentment rolling off him forced my hand.

"What do you want?" I asked.

"I heard about what happened in the tavern tonight." He held himself still. "I came to make sure one of my pack members was okay."

I shifted back a step to reveal Arrow lying on the bed. "Arrow is fine."

The Alpha's gaze flickered to the bed. "He doesn't look fine."

"Arrow is fine," I repeated and shifted the sword. "He will wake when he's ready."

"And when will that be?" Ray raised an eyebrow.

"I can't say a time."

"Why did you come to Crystal Creek?" Ray asked.

"For my mate, of course." I shifted the sword.

The Alpha's gaze didn't flinch from the swish of the water blade.

"Before you met Arrow. Did you come here for a reason? Did you know this was a shifter town?" he demanded.

The Alpha had a right to demand a newcomer's motives. I couldn't fault his leadership of his pack. Arrow had family and friends in Crystal Creek, and I'd do my best to fit in. I'd give him what he wanted.

"I assumed you were human. You've managed to blend well. I didn't recognize you were wolf shifters." I relaxed my stance a fraction. "Traveling here was a fluke. I didn't choose the location, my powers did. As for my reason, well, I required a certain gratification."

"You came here for sex." Sledge laughed and placed a hand on his stomach as his rumbling laughter grew.

"Aye." I lowered the sword.

"Quit your laughing, son." Ray slapped a hand to Sledge's shoulder. "Arrow's the best captain of the firefighters we've ever had."

I grimaced and dissolved my water sword. After the harshness of the wildfire, the Alpha's concerns were warranted. I didn't want Arrow to succumb to the Quiet either.

"Arrow asked me to mark him."

The Alpha's and Sledge's shoulders relaxed.

"Yes, I heard." Ray sighed. "You'll have to step up and take his place for a while, son."

"Sure." Sledge stepped into the room. "I'll help Saoirse keep watch over Arrow too."

"I don't need help," I hissed and moved to Arrow's side.

"You'll have to rest sometime. You're a pack member now and we take care of our pack members," Sledge said.

"Yes," Ray said. "Marianne will be along shortly, and you can arrange times to watch over Arrow until he wakes."

"Very well." I dipped my head. "I'll trust Sledge and Marianne with Arrow but no one else."

"I suppose that's understandable. We'll have to leave the official pack introduction until Arrow can present you as his mate."

"I'm not leaving his side, and I'll permit no one else to be near him." Water swirled over my hand, the sword itching to form. I kept it back with willpower. I wouldn't fit in if I kept threatening the Alpha with a sword.

"Yes, yes." Ray backed up from the doorway as though sensing the power in my hand was throbbing for release. "I'll leave Arrow's care to his mate."

"I will care for him as a mate should." The water dissipated from my hand in a whoosh.

Ray nodded and exited Arrow's house. Sledge crossed the space of the room and settled on the bed next to Arrow kicking his feet up onto the mattress and studying the room.

"We'll need to do a bit of redecorating in this room," he said. "A television there." He pointed. "And a chair."

Arms crossed, I said, "I like Arrow's bedroom as is."

"I bet you do." Sledge smirked.

"You're incorrigible."

"The sword thing you did was so cool. How did you do it?"

"With my powers."

"Sweet. So, you know how to sword fight?"

"I do."

"Awesome. Can you teach me?"

An orchid bouquet bloomed in front of the window in Arrow's bedroom. I'd added flowering plants to Arrow's house while he'd been in the Quiet. Seemed fair since Sledge had been insistent on adding furniture to Arrow's bedroom to make himself comfortable. The house felt even more like my home even with Sledge invading our personal space and making no apologies about it. I couldn't fault his protection of his friend.

"Wake up, sleeping beauty." I brushed a hand over Arrow's brow, down his cheek, and across his soft lips.

Lips I'd softly kissed many times in the two months with no response from Arrow.

"For fuck's sake, Saoirse, stop playing with him like that while I'm in the room," Sledge said.

"I can't help it. I need to touch my mate. It's a burning need to soothe him." I stroked my thumb over his lower lip.

A knock rapped on the front door.

"About time," Sledge said. "Go, get out of here. I'll look after sleeping ugly while you go for a swim with Marianne."

I swiped my hand to Arrow's chest over the swirl of knots, my Fae mating mark which caused him to remain in the Quiet.

"Thank you," I said before leaving my mate in the care of his best friend.

Marianne waited for me outside on the porch.

"How's my boy today?" she asked, gazing into the forest.

"The same," I replied. The same reply for the last two months. At this stage, I believed Arrow would be in the Quiet for many years.

"And your boy?" She dropped her gaze to my growing stomach.

"He's eager for his daily swim."

Marianne smiled. "Let's head to the waterfall then, shall we?"

I stepped off the porch and followed the now familiar track to the waterfall with Marianne by my side. Over the last two months, she'd escorted me to the waterfall to swim, to release my pent-up power over longing for Arrow. For the baby too. He loved the waterfall and when I used my power. Each time we swam he grew stronger.

The scent of the eucalyptus trees wafted all around us. Since the fire had blazed its path of destruction through the forest, life had sprung back on the blackened limbs. New shoots of green sprouted from the black-brown soil as the gentle rains of fall returned life. The seasons were changing, and for the first time in centuries, I experienced it.

A soft misting rain drifted down on us from the gray clouds over our heads. I lifted my face to the sky and reveled in the power behind the rain.

Marianne shook her head at my love of the rain. She raced ahead and ducked into the clearing around the waterfall before scampering into the side of the rocks and finding shelter. I lifted my dress over my head and dropped the pink material to the ground. It made no difference to me what the outside temperature of Earth was. I didn't experience the cold, or heat, but the rain made all the difference to the Fae power inside me. I danced and played with the rain, launching shoots of water from the waterfall and turning them into swirls before dumping them into the pool in a big splash.

The baby kicked my stomach. I placed a hand on his little mound and waded into the water. A sigh left my lips. I should feel guilty for leaving Arrow to play in the water, but the baby and I loved it so. I stayed for as long as possible until the gloomy day grew darker still with the impending fall of night.

Marianne waited with my dress in her hands. I left the water and slid on the damp garment. With a slash of my hand, I sent one last playful spray of the water across the pool and retraced my steps to home.

Home, and Arrow. My mate. If only he'd wake soon.

"Feel better now?" Marianne asked.

"Aye." I shifted a damp branch out of the way and walked through the forest.

"I've always believed our waterfall to be special, but seeing you play in it with your power, it's plain to see you're the special one."

"Thank you, Marianne." I dipped my head.

"Do you think Arrow will come back to us soon?"

"I wished I knew. He has three hundred years of memories to absorb. It may take a while."

"It's astounding to learn that's how Fae mark their mates. You'll have no secrets from him now."

"I wouldn't want there to be any secrets between us. He's my fated mate. He deserves to understand everything there is about me. I wish I could learn everything about him."

Drops of eucalyptus-scented water dripped from the trees onto my face.

"He'll tell you everything when he wakes. Wolf shifters don't keep things from their mates either. It's not such a powerful marking, but I'm sure you can sense the bond in his bite."

"Aye, I sense Arrow in the mark on my neck." I touched a hand to the mark. How I longed to experience his bite again.

Shadows stalked around us. Gray shapes I was accustomed to over the last two months, members of the wolf pack keeping guard from a distance. They never ventured close enough for me to feel threatened. I sensed their inquisitiveness, but I was adamant they stay away until Arrow woke, and they respected my wishes.

We arrived at the cabin and continued to the bedroom. Marianne checked on Arrow every day after my swim and sat with him while I ate dinner with Sledge, who I'd found, to my surprise, a humorous companion in this stressful time. His brash self-assured attitude was larger than life and made me laugh. Much like his first pickup line he'd said to me. Although, now, he was more like a brother since he was Arrow's best friend and he respected our mating. Strange to think I might have used him for sex the night I'd slipped through the veil in my heat.

Loud fighting sounds echoed from the bedroom. I rolled my eyes. From the first day of Arrow's drift in the Quiet, Sledge shifted a television into the bedroom and played video games while he sat with Arrow. I didn't object, but I insulted his sword fighting skills when watching him play the video games.

"Looks like you're about to lose," I said hovering over Sledge's shoulder.

Marianne sat beside Arrow on the bed.

"Stop looking over my shoulder," Sledge said.

"He's got you on the run. You need to... never mind."

"Damn it." Sledge tossed the game controller aside.

I patted his muscular arm in commiseration. "Tomorrow I'll show you how to counteract that strike."

"Good, I get to swing a sword at you." He grinned.

"You'll do no such thing," Arrow said.

We turned to stare at Arrow. My mouth dropped open. He'd spoken. His eyes were closed. *Did I hear things?* There was no sign he'd spoken. He appeared in the Quiet still. I snapped my mouth shut.

Marianne gazed at Arrow with tears shining in her eyes.

I turned my gaze to Sledge. *Did he hear Arrow too?* Sledge's mouth hung open, his eyes wide. Maybe I didn't hear things. My heart beat a rapid cadence inside my chest. I dug my fingers into Sledge's arm.

"Stop touching, Sledge, honey, before I have to punch my best friend," Arrow mumbled.

"Arrow?" I gasped.

I let go of Sledge's arm and raced to the bed, throwing myself on top of Arrow and peppering kisses over his face. Marianne shifted off the bed, but I didn't pay her any heed. Arrow's golden eyes glowing at me with so much emotion and longing held me captive. He let me kiss him again and again, his forehead, his cheeks, his eyebrows, his nose, his lips, everywhere my lips touched wasn't enough. I'd never get enough of Arrow.

He threaded his fingers into my hair and held my head still to his searching lips. They met mine in the most soul-rending kiss I'd ever experienced. His lips and tongue marked me as his. I marked him back with my lips and tongue. No one or nothing would ever stand between us again.

I stroked my hand to my mark on his chest. The swirl of knots heated with my touch, grew in intensity until we gasped for breath and parted lips.

"My mate." I smiled.

CHAPTER TWENTY-THREE
ARROW

O F ALL THE WORDS I wanted to hear from Saoirse, she said the very ones I'd dreamed about. *My mate.*

"Hey, mate, yourself," I said and grinned.

I ran a hand down her body and rubbed the bump in her stomach. Our boy was bigger than when she'd marked me. *How long was I lost in Saoirse's memories?* I'd watched the joy she'd experienced growing up inside the Fae royal palace with her brothers and sisters. The way her grandparents had doted on her. And the devastation she'd suffered from their loss. The bright flare of flames the day she'd stepped through the veil by her father's side to find them burned at the stake. I rubbed my chest over the mark. I'd felt her pain then and now. That pain would never go away for her. But then her father had gathered his remaining family and kept them safe. I understood his fears now. Why he'd been so against our mating. Against Saoirse living on Earth. But I'd protect her.

Nothing would get through me and hurt my mate.

No mortal or immortal.

She'd had a pleasant life locked inside the Summer Court, but I'd sensed her need for more during those years in her memories. The need for someone to love her as a mate. She had that now.

"He's bigger."

"He is."

I rolled Saoirse over onto her back and gazed down at her expanding middle with awe and regret I'd missed out on time with her.

"How long was I out?"

"Two months," Mom said.

"Yeah, a shitty two months without my best mate," Sledge said.

I dragged my gaze from the woman who meant the world to me and studied my mom and best friend. Neither of them appeared happy with me.

"Sorry." I shrugged.

Mom huffed. "Two months and that's the first thing you say to your mother?"

I rose from the bed and hugged her.

"Better," she said hugging me back.

I ended the hug and slapped a macho hug on Sledge, who slapped me on the back.

"Good to have you back," he said. "I can hand back captaincy of the firefighters now."

"Good to be back." I stepped over to the bed, sunk onto the mattress next to Saoirse and drew her into my arms. "What'd I miss? Besides the obvious." I rubbed her growing stomach. "How's the little fella?"

"He's good," Saoirse said and bit her lip. "I'm surprised, yet hopeful he'll make it."

"Of course, he will, honey, he's got the stubborn wolf shifter gene," I said.

"Your mom believes that too."

"Are you okay after your little siesta?" Sledge folded his arms over his chest.

"Little siesta." I laughed. "It didn't feel like sleep. It was like I lived every one of those three hundred and thirty-four years of your life, Saoirse. Why didn't you tell me you were so old?"

"Cougar, hey?" Sledge winked.

"Shut up, Sledge." Saoirse threw a pillow at him.

Sledge dodged the flying pillow with ease and laughed.

"I see you two have become friends." I eyed my mate and my best friend.

"No need to be jealous, buddy," Sledge said. "She's all yours, but she is exceptional with a sword."

"Yeah, I overheard your comment, and there'll be no sword fighting with my mate, in particular, while she's pregnant."

"I'm not an invalid, Arrow." Saoirse wriggled in my arms.

Still, I held her.

"I fought my father and won. No one is a better swordsman than him."

"I saw that, Saoirse." My body shuddered at the memory. "I saw so many things." I rubbed a hand through her hair loving the silkiness running through my fingers. Then I buried my nose into one of her flowers and inhaled the fresh scent of the first rains that always drifted from her.

"So, you know I'm capable of teaching Sledge to fight with a sword." Her spine stiffened.

She was capable of so much more. Her skills astounded me. She enthralled me. This beautiful woman, powerful Fae, and a princess was my fated mate.

"You'll never win an argument against your mate, Arrow," Mom said. "You may as well let her continue to teach Sledge or you'll make your life a living hell."

I rubbed my brow. The images of Saoirse and her sword fights flashed through my mind. The scenes made me shudder, but she was talented, adept, and skilled with the sword.

"Fine," I huffed.

Sledge made a whipping sound.

"Piss off, Sledge," I groused. "You wait until you're mated, I'm going to give you so much shit and make your mate sword fight with me."

"You don't know how to sword fight." Sledge's eyes twinkled.

"Saoirse will teach me, won't you, honey?"

"For sure." She nodded.

"That's my mate." I grinned.

"And you're mine," she said.

We grinned at each other like lovesick wolf pups. I loved her. Everything about her. Everything I'd learned about her life. Her family. The Fae's struggles in the past and the current. Saoirse was strong. She was beautiful. She was mine. I brushed my thumb over her lips.

Saoirse parted them for me.

"We'll see you both tomorrow," Mom said and tugged Sledge's arm dragging him out of our bedroom.

The front door shut, but I'd already captured Saoirse's lips with mine.

She opened to me in the way she always did, with heat and passion. The wildness of the wolf inside me glowed in happiness. Saoirse was perfect for me in every way. The fact I'd doubted she'd wanted me filled me with horror I'd entertained the idea for even a second. I had no doubts now. Her mark wiped any doubts in my mind. I'd show her for eternity my doubts would never enter my head again.

I shifted her from my lap and laid her on the bed with reverence.

"Watching you go through all those years and seeing how fiercely protective you are. How soft your heart is toward your family..."

She cupped my face.

"I'm honored you gave them up for me."

"I'd give anything up for you." She stroked her thumbs over my hairy cheeks. "I've waited a long time for a fated mate."

"I realize that now. I'm sorry I doubted you wanted me."

She sighed. "I didn't give you any reason to think I did."

"I should have known though and sensed it as your mate."

"How does my mark feel?" She shifted her hands to my bare chest and traced the mark of swirled knots etched into my skin over my heart.

"It's warm, powerful, like you."

"I'm sorry I hurt you when I marked you." She kissed my chest.

"I'd take the pain of a thousand markings for you."

She giggled. "Exaggerate much?"

I shuffled down her body dropping kisses to her neck, to the front of her dress, and over the bulge of our baby in her stomach. I lingered there for a few minutes pressing kisses over and over.

Saoirse's eyes grew hooded with desire. Her lusty scent drifted from between her legs. My wolf rumbled in satisfaction. He wanted to taste her. I wanted to taste her. When I eased her dress up her legs, I found her wearing panties.

I lifted my head in shock.

She laughed. "I swam at the waterfall with your mom. I couldn't very well swim naked."

"No, I should hope not." I ripped the panties from her body and buried my nose in her heat.

"Arrow," she moaned.

I spread her legs and devoured her with the hunger of a man starved for months of food. I suppose it was the truth. And she was my favorite food. My favorite taste. Her sweet honey coated my tongue. I buried deeper into her damp folds and licked her to her first orgasm of the night. Her legs quaked over my shoulders and clamped around my ears. I fluttered my tongue against her hard nub prolonging the pleasure for her. I'd happily eat her all day and night with the soft moans coming from her mouth. She gave one last shudder and sigh before flopping her head back on the bed.

I shifted back and stared at her flushed pink opening welcoming me with her scent, her heat, and her moisture. Saoirse peered down the length of her body at me. I traced a finger around the softness of her opening, circling the place I wanted to bury my hard dick and never leave.

She wriggled her hips and sought to force me inside. Instead, I kept up my slow circling, brushing the hard nub of her clit on each circle until she panted and writhed.

"Arrow, I need you inside me." She moaned.

"I need to be inside you too, honey."

I buried my tongue inside her greedy opening, feeling her clamp around my tongue and buck against my face as her sweetness gushed over my tongue. Her inner muscles clenched and unclenched against my probing as another orgasm rippled from her sweet pussy. I flipped her over, yanked her hips up, and buried my throbbing dick into her welcoming heat with a roar.

"Aye," she moaned.

I tugged her hair to the side with my fist and buried my teeth into the back of her neck. She gasped in a delighted moan. I pumped my hips hard and deep.

"Don't stop," she begged. "I need you, Arrow."

The best sound to my ears. Her pants and moans spurred me on harder. My hips thrust in a mind of their own, lost in the pleasure of my mate's body, in her wetness, in the tightness of her sheath, in the building of her orgasm and mine.

My balls pulled up tighter, the pressure built. I needed to experience her release on my cock. I found her clit with my fingers and strummed the hard nub in firm circles feeling her clench tighter and tighter until I believed she'd strangle my orgasm from me. Then she rippled in pleasure sending my eyes rolling back in my head and a howl from my lungs. The pressure inside me released a hot spurt inside her sheath.

I pumped my hips deliberately and dragged the contracting ripples of pleasure from Saoirse and myself to the longest orgasm of my life.

She fell to the bed, and I followed her with my arms still wrapped around her. My cock growing hard already. Once wouldn't be enough. Twice wouldn't be enough.

My mate was in for a long night of pleasure.

CHAPTER TWENTY-FOUR

ARROW

A FEW WEEKS LATER, when we spent more than an hour without stripping each other of any attempt at clothing and pleasuring each other until we laid in a pile of panting sweaty limbs, I accepted the invitation to introduce my mate to the pack.

A flower dropped from Saoirse's hair and landed on her lap in my Ranger. I collected the small bloom, sniffed the petals, and tucked the flower into my pocket for safekeeping.

"How many of my flowers do you have?"

I shrugged.

"Mates don't keep secrets."

Saoirse twisted the folds of her dress in her fingers. She'd admitted to being nervous about meeting the pack tonight. I'd comforted her as best I could with words that she had nothing to be nervous about.

"Sixteen," I said.

"I realized you counted them, but I don't understand why."

"Why I keep them or why I count them?" I asked.

"Both."

"They're a little piece of you, of course, I'd keep them. As for counting them, I'm not sure." I flicked her a glance before keeping my attention on the dirt road.

"You're counting them as a way of keeping track of our time together." She released the twisted fabric. "You don't need to worry, I'm never leaving you again."

I trusted her she'd never leave me, not now our mating marks connected us.

"Do you miss your family?"

"Aye," she whispered.

"Your family must miss you too."

"I'm worried about them, Arrow. I need to help them even though I can't go back to the Summer Court."

My hand clasped hers. "We'll help your family. Eloise's great gran knew a Fae. We'll talk to her tonight."

Saoirse growled.

"Easy, honey." I chuckled. "Anyone would think you're a wolf shifter."

"That woman placed her hands on you," she stated like it was the most obvious reason in the world.

As much as her protective jealousy warmed my heart, I never wanted her to worry about another woman.

"She'll never have them on me again. I'll never allow it to happen again," I stated. "I wasn't in my right mind before."

"And your mind is right now?"

"My mind is never better knowing you so well. I've studied your memories. I think you're right about your spring's decline affecting your reproduction."

"You do?" She let out a relieved breath. "I could convince no one they were connected."

"They're idiots then."

She laughed, a light tinkling sound of happiness. "If you ever meet them, don't call them idiots. Above all, Lorcan. He believes he's the smartest."

"Lorcan, hmm, he's quite impressive with his fire, but nowhere near as amazing as you with your water."

"You're such a sweet talker."

I parked the truck in the town square in front of the town hall. Our first official trip into the center of town as mates. The town hall greeted us with its large arched entrance of dusky white-gray stone bricks and on top a tower housing a clock.

I opened the door for Saoirse. "They built the town hall in the late 1800s."

"It's spectacular."

"Not as spectacular as your palace."

"Intimidated of the palace?" She raised her eyebrow.

"A little. And you're a princess." I drew her into my arms and nuzzled her hair. "But you're mine."

"I am. Princess or not. I'm intimidated by your wolf pack." She wrapped her arms around my waist and clung onto me.

"You haven't even met them yet."

"I have. When the fire blazed through the forest."

I peered down at her. "When you saved them from the fire you mean."

"Aye." She ducked her head.

I didn't want to remember the rest of the day when the Fae King froze me in a block of ice and imprisoned my mate in the Summer Court. The day I'd thought I'd lost my mate forever. I had her in my arms now and no one would ever take her from me again.

"Come on." I wrapped my arm around her waist and walked my mate inside the building under the great stone arches. "Mom can't wait to show you off."

"I like your mom." Saoirse slipped her fingers into the belt loops on my jeans.

"She likes you too. So does Sledge, and my other team members. I wish you'd got to know the twins before they left. They were always playing practical jokes."

"You're not happy with the Alpha," she noted.

"No, I'm not." My arm tightened around her waist on its own.

"Will it cause problems for us?"

Mom swooped upon us and hauled us into a hug before I could answer. "I'm so glad you both came. Everyone is looking forward to meeting the Fae princess who saved them."

Saoirse ducked her head and brushed her hair with trembling fingers.

"Let me introduce you," I said.

Wolf shifter after wolf shifter walked in front of us. Saoirse's face was a mask in a polite smile and concentration as she memorized the names and faces of the pack. They were all so nice and thankful to my mate, as they should be. They treated her as a revered princess with a gentle touch of gratitude on her hand.

The last man to greet us was the Alpha.

"Saoirse, this is the pack Alpha, Ray Braidwood," I said.

"We've met." Saoirse dipped a greeting.

"Welcome to the pack, Saoirse."

"Thank you for your warm welcome," Saoirse said.

"All mates have to be accepted into the pack." He waved his meaty hands.

I stood up straighter.

Saoirse placed a calming hand on my arm.

"Arrow's my mate. He's told me in significant detail of the town and how a witch's spell protects it. I won't reveal that secret. He also said how you all look out for each other, of the families and friendships formed here dating back a long time. Fae and wolf shifters are not so different. We each like to protect our people. Arrow told me you've protected yours."

Ray nodded, his gaze reassessing me. "Congratulations on the new pup."

"Thank you," I said and dropped a possessive hand to my mate's stomach. "He's doing well on Earth."

"He'll do well in our pack. I look forward to meeting our latest pack member." He smiled.

The baby kicked under my palm in Saoirse's stomach. I gazed down in wonder at the power of our son.

"He likes your words," I said.

"He's part wolf shifter he can hear the truth in my words," the Alpha said.

I let my hostility over Lyle's and Kirk's relocation go. If they weren't happy with their new location, we would have heard from them by now. The Alpha accepted us into his pack, and I wanted a secure family for Saoirse and our baby to grow up surrounded by love and acceptance since she'd given up her family to form ours.

"Food's up," Sledge shouted from the other side of the room.

"That son of mine." Ray shook his head.

"He's outstanding," Saoirse said. "A loyal friend. You must be proud of him."

The Alpha shot her a look and tilted his head. "Let's eat and enjoy the rest of the night. The band will play after dinner. Perhaps Arrow will permit me to have a dance with a princess?"

I frowned, and said, "That's up to my mate."

The Alpha nodded and walked over to the long table set with tray after tray of food. A mountain of meat and vegetables for my vegetarian mate.

"You handled him well," I whispered in Saoirse's ear and led her over to the table.

"I learned how to handle my father for the most part. Your Alpha is a pussycat compared to the Fae King."

I roared with laughter. "Shh, don't say the 'c' word around a pack of wolves. You might start a race to catch one."

"You're terrible." She nudged my arm with her elbow.

"Don't believe me? Yell out cat and see what happens."

"And have everyone race off from our party?" Her eyes glittered in amusement.

"Then I'd have you alone to myself," I said huskily.

"Ah, now I understand your plan." She grinned.

"As if you didn't already."

"Aye, my mate, I understand your plan, and I'm looking forward to it tonight." She squeezed my ass and picked up a plate. "Eating, dancing—"

"Fucking." I breathed into her ear.

Goosebumps broke out on her neck. "Aye, that too."

"Eloise went to the restroom by herself," Sledge said sliding into my side.

Eloise had avoided me and Saoirse all night. I couldn't fault her hesitation after her humiliation in the tavern. Also, the power vibrating from Saoirse whenever she caught sight of her would put anyone off. A part of me wanted to see Saoirse whip her ass with her water magic. She never ceased to amaze me with what she achieved with water. Her water swords were phenomenal, and Sledge agreed.

Despite my wolf raging at me to not allow Saoirse to train Sledge to sword fight, I joined them. After seeing her entire life, I knew with a certainty she wouldn't put herself in any danger training us. She was too much of a master to allow any harm to come to her or our baby. She'd incapacitated her father and from her memories,

I'd seen that was the only time she'd outmaneuvered him with a sword. The one time she'd fought him to get back to me. I didn't doubt her conviction to be my mate.

I risked a glance at Saoirse who was otherwise preoccupied with my mom and a handful of elder pack members. She enthralled them. They gazed at her in awe. As fascinated by her powers as I was. Add in the fact she was a Fae princess, and they were gob smacked. Many from our pack didn't harbor the resentments of the old, and the few holding onto them, well, I'd make sure they accepted Saoirse.

"Let's do this now." I nodded.

We stalked from the main room down the hallway to the restrooms and waited for Eloise to emerge. The door swung open, and she ground to a halt.

"Shit," she said.

Sledge grinned. I stalked closer.

"Eloise," I said.

"Look, Arrow, I'm sorry if I caused offense."

"You did." I scowled. "Why would you try to take another's mate?"

She brushed a hand through her long dark hair. "We don't have many men where I come from. We've learned to fight for them."

Her words rang true to my ears, but I'd never trust her.

"You understand, there's no chance with me."

She waved a hand at my chest. "Not now you carry her mark."

"Not before even." I narrowed my eyes. "A wolf mating is for life. You should grasp how mating works."

She glanced away.

Sledge slung an arm around my shoulders and leaned toward Eloise. "What else can you tell us about the Fae?"

She started with a blink of her eyes and a twitch of her lips, so slight if we hadn't been watching her, we would have missed the telling spasm.

"Not much." She met our gazes.

Liar.

Sledge repositioned his arm from my shoulders to hers. "Eloise, sweet thing, you can tell us."

I stifled a snort. Sweet thing my ass.

She gazed up at Sledge and moistened her lips.

"I'm looking for a mate, Sledge." Eloise slid her hand to his chest.

Sledge removed her hand and stepped back. "Sorry, I'm not interested in a mate."

"Too bad." She pouted. "You were my second choice in this pack."

Sledge's muscles tensed. "Guess you'll have to settle on your third choice."

I flicked a glance at Sledge before settling on Eloise. My dislike for Eloise grew by the second.

"Eloise," I snapped with a show of teeth. "What do you know about the Fae?"

She huffed. "The Fae have immense powers. There is nothing they can't do."

"What about their heritage?"

She pointed at my chest where Saoirse's mating mark etched my skin. "You know more than I'll ever know."

How did she realize the location of the mark?

"Eloise, there you are," Clara called. "The dancing is starting."

"Coming." She brushed past us. "See you around town."

We watched her meet up with her friend. The pair scurried down the hallway, cast a glance over their shoulders at us, and rounded the corner disappearing from our sight.

"I don't trust her," Sledge said.

"My sentiments exactly. She knows something, and she's not telling us."

"We'll figure it out." Sledge slapped a hand on my back. "For tonight, let's enjoy your party and the fact my dad accepted Saoirse into the pack."

I grinned. My mate. My pack. All together as it should be. With everyone by my side, then we'd help Saoirse and her family. They were now a part of my family. Together we'd be stronger and our baby needed both families. *Who would teach our child the way of the Fae if her family weren't around?*

I'd do everything I could to see that come to pass.

We returned to the main room. Saoirse glided across the floor in her long floaty pink gown, the ones she loved to wear, the ones I loved to see her wear. She looked regal, with her flower crown and glowing beauty. No one compared to my mate.

I swept her into my arms. "Dance with me."

She fell into my embrace in an instant, easy, acceptance of her place in my arms, and let me sweep her onto the dance floor. Our bodies swayed in perfect harmony of two mates who knew the other as well as they knew themselves.

"You're glowing tonight." I eased her closer until our hips rested together swaying to the rhythm of the music. "My beautiful mate, I can't wait to get you alone."

Saoirse smiled, her happiness shining even brighter across her face. "I can't wait for you to bend me over."

I groaned then chuckled. My mate was a perfect match for me.

CHAPTER TWENTY-FIVE
SAOIRSE

ONE MOMENT LONGER AND I wouldn't have made it through the party without self-combusting into an orgasm. All night long Arrow brushed soft tender kisses across my cheek, stroked my arms, hands, neck, and back in a light caress of his fingers. Every nerve ending in my body was on fire as though I was in heat again, but this need was all for Arrow and the emotions I'd developed for him in our short time together as mates. With the strength of my passions, it was a wonder my power hadn't rained down on every wolf shifter head in the town hall tonight.

Arrow's whispered words in my ear as we danced sending moisture into my panties. How he couldn't wait to suck my nipples into his mouth. Run his teeth over my clit. Sink his tongue deep inside me. Feel me come all over his face.

I snapped my seatbelt buckle in place sending a loud snap inside his vehicle.

Arrow chuckled even though his pants bulged under the steering wheel.

I flexed my hands. "How long until we get home?"

Arrow shrugged. "I'm taking the scenic route home to show you around the entire town since it's your first time here."

"Arrow," I moaned.

"Saoirse," he said, his golden eyes glittering in the dark.

I unclipped my seatbelt and climbed onto his lap.

"What are you doing, honey?"

"I can't wait, and neither can you by the feel."

"We can't here. Everyone inside will hear us. Wolves have great hearing."

He drew me against his chest and kissed the top of my head.

I let out a sigh and sagged into his warm embrace. He ran a soothing hand up and down my back and brushed the hair from my face to kiss me with so much emotion tears welled in my eyes.

"Saoirse, what's wrong?"

I shook my head and gulped. "Nothing. It's... I feel..." I smoothed a hand over my heart. "Here."

Arrow smiled tenderly. "Love?"

I ran my gaze over his face, the face of my mate, the face of the man I loved.

"Yes," I said. "I love you."

"Honey, I love you too."

He leaned forward to kiss me again, but a knock rapped on the car window. Arrow wound the fogged window down a crack.

"Are you two finished making out in the parking lot like teenagers?" Sledge asked.

Arrow laughed.

"What does he mean?" I asked.

"Oh, honey, I'll tell you when we get home." Amusement lit Arrow's face adding to the happiness already glowing from him.

Sledge chuckled and sauntered away.

Arrow wound the window back up. I shifted to the other seat and refastened my seatbelt.

"Let's go home," I said.

"What about a tour of the town?"

"We have plenty of time for a tour, right now I want to snuggle with you in bed all night and tell you I love you over and over."

Arrow grinned. "I can't think of anything better."

The baby kicked, and I placed a hand on my stomach.

"He agrees with you."

"Although, there is something better." Arrow started the vehicle.

"What?"

"Me telling you I love you over and over."

The baby kicked again. Strong-willed and healthy, he'd make it into this world. I believed that now. A mate's love for their fated mate was the most powerful thing in any world. Our love was powerful. Our son would be powerful too. And our love would grow endless.

"Oh, Arrow, you're stuck with me now."

He chuckled. "I couldn't think of anything better."

"In truth?"

"Yes." He leaned across the seats and kissed my forehead. "Because I'm stuck to you like honey."

I snorted. "You and Sledge need to work on your lines."

"Hey, I don't need to work on anything, I've got the woman of my dreams."

I sighed. The woman of his dreams. No one ever made me feel more special than Arrow. "Kiss me, Arrow."

He obliged. A firm kiss of his mouth against mine, then he tugged my lips with his teeth sending a shiver racing through my body. I'd never tire of his bite. It was everything. The one thing which tied us together for eternity the first time we met. He broke the kiss and met my lust-filled gaze with one of his own.

"Take me home."

"With pleasure, my mate."

EPILOGUE

M ONTHS LATER THE WINTER rain splattered on the roof, a rat at tat-tat setting my power on edge. It wanted free to dance in the rain.

"Arrow let's go for a swim."

"Honey, it's freezing outside."

"I don't feel the cold." I pressed my face to the window. Our baby was already dancing with the power of the rain. "Besides, it'll be fun."

Arrow chuckled. "It might be fun for you, but we'll get drenched in the downpour."

"I'll make it fun for you too, I promise."

"Yeah? What are you promising?"

Arrow wrapped his arms around me from behind and nuzzled the back of my neck.

"Anything you want."

"Anything, huh?"

He rubbed my rounded stomach. "Hmm, how about when we're finished playing in the rain and water, I lay you out on the rug in front of the fire and tease you until you're begging me to fuck you?"

I turned around in his arms. "You drive a hard bargain."

Arrow laughed and hauled me against his hardness. "I'm always hard for you."

I palmed the bulge in his jeans.

"Deal?" Arrow growled.

"Deal." I gave him one last firm stroke, kissed his cheek, then raced for the front door. Stepping outside into the rain, I squealed in delight and let my power free to dance with the water droplets.

"The lake or waterfall?"

"Hmm, now we have a deal, the lake is closer..."

Arrow caught me in his arms and spun me in the air. I threw my head back and laughed as drops of rain splattered over my cheeks, eyelids, and lips.

"It's getting harder to do this now your stomach is bigger," he said lowering me back to my bare feet.

I laughed and skipped through the puddles into the forest where the foliage of the trees lessened the impact of the rain. Eucalyptus-scented water dripped onto my head from the branches above and ran rivulets through my hair. Arrow covered his large hand around mine and held branches out of the way for us to pass through the forest until we arrived at the lake.

"He loves swimming." I set a hand on my stomach.

"Because you do."

"Aye," I said.

We stripped and waded into the lake. Arrow encircled me with his arms from behind and rested his chin on my shoulder and let me play with the water. His warm hands cupped our baby as though he'd protect him from anything intent on harming him. The baby moved under Arrow's hands. He loved it when his father held him.

"You know in human terms, with how far along your pregnancy has progressed, the baby could be born today and survive."

"We're not human." I stopped playing with the water and just as suddenly the rain stopped.

"Which means even better odds."

"True." I placed my hands on top of Arrow's. I'd almost lost my fear of losing the baby. He was so strong, it was hard to imagine he wouldn't fight to live. "But I'm not ready to meet him today, we have plans for the rest of the day."

Arrow chuckled.

"I love you, Arrow."

"I love you too, Saoirse."

He kissed me with the passion and lust I reciprocated. A tug of lips, a slide of tongues, a nip of teeth.

"Are you finished playing in the water?" he said against my lips. "Because I need to take you home and make you beg now."

"Aye," I begged already.

This feeling was more than my heat ever was, the intense hunger for Arrow was all for him and I never had to wonder if it was the pheromones from my heat making him want me. He wanted me with the same intensity now as he did when I was in heat.

He wanted me for me.

And I loved him even more for it.

A fated mate was better than I'd imagined.

The forest trees rustled as birds took flight. A woman ran onto the shore casting a glance behind her.

Briana?

Sledge's large black wolf exploded from the trees. The pair faced off against each other. What was Briana doing here? And why was Sledge chasing her?

"Arrow, stop Sledge before my sister hurts him."

"Your sister?" His eyebrows rose. "Why would she hurt Sledge?"

"Why is he chasing her?"

"You have a point. I'll go ask him." He dropped a peck to my forehead. "Don't worry I won't let anything happen to either of them."

Arrow raced through the water changing into his golden wolf. A sense of pride rolled through me that he was mine. This man. Wolf shifter would protect me from anything. I trusted him to protect those I loved too.

For whatever came next with my family, we were in this together as fated mates.

FATED MATES OF THE FAE ROYALS

1. Fae's Song

2. Fae's Wolf

3. Fae's Alpha

4. Fae's Heart

5. Fae's Witch

6. Fae's Dream

7. Fae's Fate

8. Fae's Love

ACKNOWLEDGMENTS

First, thank you to my family for putting up with me disappearing into the world of books. To Belinda, thank you for encouraging me to write again after I lost everything in a computer crash. Remember to back up! A lot of work goes into creating a story, and I'm always thankful for the support of my online writing buddies, beta readers, and fellow authors, Immy for always making me smile, Tammy for believing in me from the start, Karen for being willing to read any level of heat I write. Cassie for her hand holding. Lana for her invaluable knowledge. Also, my fabulous beta reader Erica and her help with US English. The biggest thank you goes to my 'twin' Dannielle, who is the best critique partner, cheerleader, and sounding board ever, and is forever fixing my comma errors, sorry Dannielle I'm afraid you're stuck with them and me. Finally thank you to all you romance readers. You are my tribe.

ALSO BY

Anthologies

Reluctant Bride

Alpha Male

ABOUT AUTHOR

Helen Walton is a tea drinking, chocoholic, romance writer. Stories are her obsession. She adores creating sensual romances containing a sprinkling of humor and the all-important happy ending. She lives in South Australia with her family, and menagerie of quirky animals where they all take her away from her book world and demand to be fed. Lucky for them, she enjoys cooking but prefers baking.

Sign up for my newsletter for exclusive content.

https://www.helenwaltonauthor.com/newsletter

Visit my website

https://www.helenwaltonauthor.com/

Follow me

BB bookbub.com/profile/helen-walton

f facebook.com/Helen-Walton-Author-1034966677
06602/

g goodreads.com/author/show/20249188.Helen_Wa
lton

[O] instagram.com/helen.walton.author

♪ tiktok.com/@helen.walton.author